I0577631

# WITH A FRIEND LIKE YOU

## VANESSA GRAY BARTAL

DRY CREEK PRESS

Copyright 2023 Vanessa Gray Bartal

This is a work of fiction. Names, characters, places and incidents either are the product of the author's imagination or are used fictitiously. Any resemblance to actual persons, living or dead, events, or locales is entirely coincidental.

# PROLOGUE

Bronwyn sat on the patio, as close to the privet as she could get without actually being absorbed into the hedge. In front of her sat a napkin with six smuggled cookies. Beside it was a book. She was supposed to be mingling. She was supposed to be on a diet. She was supposed to be a lot of things.

"Psst."

Guiltily, she dropped the cookie from her fingers and sat up, looking around.

"Psst. Gimme one."

The voice was coming from behind her, seemingly from inside the hedge. Had a reporter hidden himself there? It wouldn't be the first time. Bronwyn whirled to look, squinting. From the shadows, a boy stepped out. He was a few years older than her sixteen, but she still thought of him as a boy. He was smoking.

"There's no smoking here," she informed him.

"Isn't the tobacco industry a huge supporter of your mom?" he asked. His tone was sardonic, a word she had learned recently from her literature teacher and kept using so she wouldn't forget it.

"So is the American Lung Association," she countered.

"Good point." He tossed the cigarette to the ground.

"Um, hello, you're littering on our property," she complained.

"My apologies. I'll toss it onto my property." He picked up the cigarette and flicked it to the other side of the shrub. "There we go, problem solved." He sat and filched one of her cookies.

"Hey," she said, hugging them to her like a lifeline because, at the moment, they were the only joyful thing in her life.

"Six is too many," he said.

Her eyes narrowed on him. "I've only had six hundred calories today. I'm allowed a treat."

"What are you, like a Weight Watcher's spokesperson?" he asked.

Bronwyn winced.

He rolled his eyes. "Kid, that wasn't an insult. You're not fat. The press has it wrong on that count."

She frowned and set the napkin of cookies aside. He picked them up again and shoved them into her hands.

"I'm not supposed to be talking to you," she muttered.

"Why not?"

"Because you're the enemy," she said. He was the son of her mother's political rival, next door neighbor, and polar opposite. Her mother had recently won his mother's seat in congress. His mother wanted it back and was out for blood. Bronwyn wracked her brain, trying to remember his name, and then it came to her: Julian.

"Who says?"

"Everyone. My mom, your mom, the media. Everyone."

"I'm going to clue you in on something: you're talking to Roger Clinton, Billy Carter, and Rosemary Kennedy all rolled into one handsome package."

"What's that supposed to mean?" she asked.

"It means," he began as he stole another of her precious cookies and ate it, not bothering to chew with his mouth closed or disguise the chocolate cookie mess now masticating between his jaws, "I'm the official family screw-up. The good news is the pressure's off. I can do whatever I want. Something for you to consider."

She frowned. "What's that supposed to mean?"

"Where are you brothers and sisters?" he asked.

Her frown deepened to a scowl. "Mingling."

He tilted his head at her as if to say, *See.*

"I am not a screw-up," Bronwyn said, but inside her chest something shifted. Was she the Roger Clinton of her family or whatever the conservative version of that might be? Did Reagan have a screw-up sibling?

"Nothing wrong with being a screw-up," he said.

"But I'm not." Bronwyn said and then, to her horror, burst into tears.

Julian sighed, took the napkin out of her fingers, set it on the ground, pulled her to him, and kissed her. To her further surprise, she kissed him back, plunging her fingers into his hair and pressing hungrily against him for a moment until the kiss ended and he sat back.

"Why did you do that?" she whispered, blinking at him in confusion. He was too old for her, nineteen if her math was correct. She had seen him dozens of times but never once talked to him, and he was her enemy, even if he tried to deny it. If her mother knew what just happened…

"Because why not?" he said. He reached to the ground, took another cookie from the napkin, sat up, brushed his lips softly to hers, and hopped back over the hedge, disappearing into the night as silently as he'd arrived.

# CHAPTER 1

"I'm afraid we're going to have to let you go."

"You're firing me?" Bronwyn sat rigidly still, her hands clasped tightly in her lap.

"No, no, no, of course not," her boss, Lewis, said.

"So I can keep working here?" she clarified.

"No," he said. "But you're not being fired. It's merely that we're redistributing our assets, allocating funds in other places where they take greater precedent."

She tilted her head at him like a golden retriever whose owner was unwrapping a slice of cheese. "Huh?"

He sighed. "It's not working out, Bronwyn."

"Why not?" she asked. Her throat was doing the thing again where it sealed shut, clogging with tears. *Don't cry, don't cry, don't cry,* she warned herself. *Big girls don't cry.* For some it was a song; for Bronwyn it was a life motto.

"We feel like your particular skills and talents would be a better fit somewhere else," Lewis said.

"But I don't have any skills or talents," Bronwyn countered.

He pinched the bridge of his nose. "I know."

"Oh," Bronwyn said. She thought she was doing okay at her job. Apparently not. She stood. Lewis put out a hand.

"Please don't tell your mom it ended badly."

"She won't take it out on you," Bronwyn assured him. She turned to go, briefly wondering how she would face her friends in the office. Then she remembered—she didn't have any friends in the office. No one watched her walk from Lewis's office. No one noticed when she boxed up her meager personal items and carried them to the elevator. Not one person stopped her, said goodbye, or even seemed to notice her presence in the building.

All she wanted was to go home and have a good cry but, like everything in her life, it wasn't meant to be. For one thing, she started to cry as soon as she stepped outside. Her tears were silent, but they were ugly. She had never been able to accomplish a pretty cry. Her face turned immediately puce and began leaking from all orifices. And the box was too heavy to allow her to wipe her nose or eyes. Her nose stuffed immediately, and she was forced to open her mouth to breathe. A gnat flew in, and she sputtered and choked, adding to the glory of her appearance.

No cab would stop for her in this condition. She was forced to take the Metro at rush hour. She stood with the other straphangers, except her box was too heavy to allow her to grab on to a strap. She tried to brace her feet against the floor and failed mightily, bashing her head against both the pole in front of her and the pole behind her when the train took off.

The walk from the Metro to her apartment was long, made longer by a sudden rain shower. She arrived at her apartment sopping, weeping, exhausted, and encountered all of her possessions sprawled haphazardly in the hallway.

With mounting dread, she set down her workbox and knocked on the door. "Cecily, it's me, Bronwyn."

"Go away, Bronwyn."

"What are you talking about? I live here."

"No, you don't, not anymore."

"What? You can't kick me out."

Cecily opened the door. The chain was on, and she peered through the door. "Two weeks, Bronwyn. That's how long you were supposed to be here until you found a new place. It's been two years."

"Yes, but you can't toss my stuff in the hall with no warning," Bronwyn complained, waving her hand to indicate the mess in the corridor, the mess that was her life.

"No warning? I've been warning you for months my sister was coming here to live with me. I said it in person, I sent you emails, left voicemails, texted, taped a letter on the bathroom mirror, and hired a singing telegram as a reminder."

"That was you?" Bronwyn said. She took a shaky breath. "I get it, you want me to go. I'll leave as soon as I can find a new place, but I have nowhere to go. I have nowhere to sleep tonight. I'm literally homeless."

Cecily regarded her, scanning her up and down. Bronwyn tried to look as pathetic as possible, something that took zero effort. For a moment, she thought Cecily would waiver. And then she spoke. "I don't care." The door slammed, and the bolt turned.

Bronwyn stared at her possessions. What among them did she actually need or want? She took a small suitcase, packed her toiletries and a few pairs of underwear, and left the rest behind, including her work box. Her mind was suddenly decided. She knew what she was going to do, and she wouldn't need possessions where she was going.

Resolved, she went to find her car, feeling almost cheerful now. When Bronwyn was little, she had a cat that became sick, and then sicker and sicker. Her dad wanted to put it down, to end its suffering. Bronwyn resisted, for selfish reasons, she now realized. When she finally allowed the cat to be taken to the vet, it was a relief for everyone. Now Bronwyn was the cat. Her life had become a parody. It was time she put everyone out of their misery and end it.

She trekked to her car, feeling lighthearted. It was almost over. All she had to do was find a safe place for the inevitable, and she'd be golden. And she knew the perfect spot, somewhere both deserted and familiar, the only place that had ever really felt like home, her parents' summer home along the Potomac in Virginia. She drove there by rote, not minding the heavy DC traffic for once, singing along loudly with the radio.

The house was empty, as she knew it would be. Her parents were on the campaign trail. Her siblings were leading their fabulous lives in fabulous locales. The housekeeper was part time and would likely be the one to find her in a few days. That gave Bronwyn pause. She liked Louisa, always had. In fact she had felt closer to Louisa than she ever had to her own mother, but when she thought of it that way, she supposed it was appropriate Louisa be the one to find her. She would rather it be someone who might feel a trace of actual remorse at her loss. Her mother would simply be concerned with the optics and the bad press it would bring, especially during campaign season. Then again, she would likely find a way to spin it in her favor, to garner the sympathy vote. Maybe for once in her life Bronwyn could finally do something right in her mother's eyes, to help her with her campaign instead of hinder it.

She left her belongings in the car because what was the point of bringing them inside? The house felt closed up and musty. Bronwyn sneezed. She turned on lights, opened curtains, and breezed out to the patio where the air, while humid and heavy, at least smelled natural and fresh.

She sat in what had become her spot, a shady little grove so far back it almost didn't exist. It was like a metaphor for her entire life— forgotten, unimportant, unnecessary. For a moment she sat still and breathed, letting the peace of the night wash over her. These were likely her last few moments on earth; she wanted to make sure they were good. And they were.

Resolved once again, she picked up the razor blade and held it to her wrist. *Here we go,* she thought. She took a deep breath and closed her eyes, and the hedge behind her spoke.

"You're doing it wrong."

# CHAPTER 2

Bronwyn yelped, jumped, nicked herself with the blade, and dropped it. Julian Baxter appeared from the darkness, stepping over the hedge that divided their borders. He sank wearily into the chair beside her.

"Ouch. You made me cut myself," she accused.

"I thought that was kind of the point," he said, arching one eyebrow at her in question.

"I, it…shut up," Bronwyn said. She sucked her nicked wrist into her mouth, stemming the tiny trickle of blood. Julian watched her, his expression impassive. "What are you doing here?"

"Same thing you are."

She narrowed her eyes at him. Was he attempting suicide, too? He certainly looked the part. His overgrown hair was a mess, he smelled like he hadn't showered in days, his skin had a sickly pallor to it, and he was wearing a bathrobe.

"Enjoying my parents' absentee hospitality," he added with a wry twist of his lips. "I'd ask what you're doing, but it seems rather obvious."

Bronwyn blushed, glad for the cover of night. It embarrassed her deeply he'd caught her in such a compromising moment. Then again, her life was a series of compromising moments. "What did you mean when you said I'm doing it wrong?"

"I mean you were doing it wrong."

"How can you say that when I hadn't done anything yet?" she asked.

"Because I know how it's done, and that's not it. Why are you doing it this way anyway? So messy and grotesque." He grimaced.

"I thought about pills, but I've never had a prescription," she said, and he snickered.

"A prescription. You're cute."

"Hanging seemed nice, but I'm a mess with knots, as my sailing instructor enjoyed pointing out on numerous occasions. I don't have a gun, and I'm too good a swimmer to drown myself."

"What about carbon monoxide?" he tried.

She motioned to the house. "It's a six car garage. I'd have to sit in there for days." She turned her attention to the garage, contemplating. "I probably could, though. Louisa's probably not due for a few days. That's probably a better idea. Thanks." She stood.

He put his hand on her pants and tugged her back again. "Are you insane?"

She quirked an eyebrow at him.

"Right, yes, obvious answer there, sorry. But you can't take my idea to off yourself. Do you know what kind of survivor's guilt that would leave me with? Sit down, sassy pants."

"Fine, then tell me the right way to do it this way, and I'll wait until you leave."

"I'm not your suicide coach. Geez. What's so bad about your life anyway? Because you know what they say, nothing is ever as bad as it seems."

She took a deep breath, and then she told him exactly what was wrong with her life.

He sat for a few beats in silence and said, "Well, color me wrong. Turns out your life is that bad. Here." He picked up the razor and held it out to her.

Bronwyn laughed, and then jumped in surprise. When was the last time she laughed? She couldn't remember. They sat in companionable silence a few minutes. "How's your mom's campaign going?" she asked at last.

"Literally could not care less," he said. His mother had re-won her seat in the last election, forcing her mother to try and get it back. What had once been a rivalry was now all out war, and it was uglier than it had ever been. "How's yours?"

"You really think they let me anywhere near it? I have no idea." She drummed her fingers on the table. He flattened her fingers with his palm.

"Stop that." Curiously, he didn't move his hand away, and neither did she. Instead she turned her hand slightly, clasping his fingers. He returned the slight pressure. They sat in oddly comfortable silence a long time until his stomach rumbled. "I'm hungry."

Bronwyn was too, she now realized. When was the last time she ate? Breakfast, maybe.

"Want to get something to eat?" he offered.

She grimaced. "Like go out?"

He laughed. "Uh, no." He stood, tugging her up beside him. "Come on." He dropped her hand and took a step toward his house. Bronwyn froze. She had never been there, never crossed the hedge. It was enemy territory.

Julian stepped over the hedge, realized she wasn't beside him, and turned around. "Are you coming?"

"I'm not sure I should," she said.

"It seems better than any other plans you had tonight," he said. "Why the hesitation?"

"Because of everything," she said.

"It would seem it's because of everything you're in this current condition," he said.

"Give me a better reason," she implored him.

"Because why not?" he said.

Bronwyn glanced at her parents' house behind her and licked her lips. It felt like following him would be taking a step away from everything she had ever known, but look where staying where she knew had gotten her.

When she faced Julian again, he was holding out his hand to her. Bronwyn took it and stepped over the hedge.

## CHAPTER 3

Their houses were remarkably similar. The layout was the same, but the décor differed vastly. Bronwyn's house was full of antiques and stately oil paintings. Julian's house was stuffed with modern furniture and post-modern art. She noted an original Jackson Pollock hanging over the fireplace. It was funny, kind of, the way their houses typified their entire lives. Her mother was conservative; his was liberal. Her mother enjoyed classical music and opera. Bronwyn once heard Jimmy Buffet streaming from Julian's house, and it turned out to be a live performance.

"Which one do you like better?" he asked, reading her mind as she studied the house's décor.

"Neither," Bronwyn declared before she could think of the politically correct answer.

Julian laughed. "Same."

She sat at the kitchen island while he opened the refrigerator.

"It's the same thing you said all those years ago," Bronwyn noted.

"What?" he asked absently.

"When you stepped from the hedge and kissed me, you said, 'Because why not?'"

"Ah. I guess you could say it's kind of become my life's motto," he said.

She studied his back. She had spent a lot of time over the years surreptitiously studying him. Not surprisingly, she'd had a raging crush on him after that kiss. Also not surprisingly, it had amounted to absolutely nothing. He had gone his way, and she'd gone hers, just like before. He paid no mind to her whatsoever. They hadn't spoken one word to each other since that night. Eventually she got over him, and the kiss became something like myth in her mind.

"Do you even know my name?" she asked.

He turned to her with a smile. He had a Puckish nature, and the smile reflected that. It flowed with mischief, even now in his diminished and sorry looking state. "Does it start with a D?" he guessed.

"B."

"Your name is Bea?"

She wrinkled her nose at him. "No."

He rolled his eyes. "Yes, *Bronwyn*, I know your name, *Bronwyn*. You've been my next door neighbor for thirty years, *Bronwyn*."

"Stop saying Bronwyn, you weirdo," she said, and he laughed. "And I'm only twenty seven."

"I know, I remember the day they brought you home from the hospital."

"Really?" she said.

"No. Are you crazy?"

"I think we've already covered that," she said, and he laughed again. "Are you making omelets?"

"Why, do you want an omelet?"

"No, I hate eggs. But when men in books and on TV cook, they always make an omelet."

"I'm making a quesadilla."

"How ethnic," she said.

"You can tell your mom, see if you can use it to tie up the Latinx vote."

"Shockingly, she doesn't take my suggestions anymore," Bronwyn said.

Julian smiled and commenced chopping vegetables. "You want to hear something funny?"

"Desperately."

"My mom has tied up the Latinx vote, and the black vote, and the working man's vote. But my parents own four houses and three generations ago, my great grandfather owned slaves and all our housekeepers and staff are Hispanic, and I went to an all white prep school. In fact, until college, the only ethnic minority friend I had was Carlo."

Bronwyn perked up. "You know Carlo? Louisa's son?" After her crush on Julian ended, it transferred itself to Carlo who was now a successful lawyer in DC.

"Yes, I know Carlo. He's a good friend of mine." He glanced at her. "Looks like someone else knows Carlo. Were you guys a thing at one point?"

"Not hardly. Carlo's always been out of my league."

He tipped his head at her. "He's the immigrant son of your wealthy, powerful parents' housekeeper."

"And yet still rates higher on their scale than I do because he made something of himself, pulled himself up by his bootstraps and followed the American dream. While I languished in my privilege, doing nothing, being nothing. Just floating in a haze of big, fat nothing."

"Wow, don't tell me you're single, Bronwyn, because that self-deprecating desperation is so sexy you must beat the men away with a stick."

She smiled and nabbed a piece of cheese. He used the knife to scoot another closer within her reach. Suddenly she was famished.

"Is all that stuff you said true?" she asked. She didn't know him well enough to know if he was exaggerating.

"I left a lot out but, yes."

"Wow, your mom sounds really messed up," she mused.

"Neither of our mothers believes the nonsense they spout. They're two sides of the same ambitious coin."

"My mom does."

He paused, knife held aloft, staring at her. "I don't know you well enough to know if that was sarcasm."

"It wasn't," she assured him. "She runs on a platform of family values, and our family is solid."

He gave her what she could only guess was a pitying look. "Except the daughter she treats like trash, you mean."

"That's different," Bronwyn said, waving her hand dismissively.

"How is that different? Are you not a part of her family?"

"Yes, but I'm the, what was your word, token screw-up."

"Everyone's a screw-up in one way or another. Some of us are just more obvious about it," he said.

"No, my mom really cares about the stuff she says. She really means it."

He was still paused mid-chop, staring at her. "You're actually kind and genuine, aren't you?"

"I try to be," she said, not that it mattered. She had no friends, and her family would find it a relief if she disappeared.

"How did that happen growing up here?" he asked, and he sounded sincerely curious.

"My parents are nice, good people and deep down, deep, *deep* down, I know they love me," she said.

He shook his head. "Oh, Bronwyn, you're even worse off than I suspected."

"No I'm not," she countered hotly, and he laughed.

"Yes, baby girl, you are. I thought you were shattered and disillusioned. Turns out you're merely sad. You have so much farther to fall."

"This has been an encouraging pep talk. I'm all better now, thank you."

"I'm no one's idea of a life coach." He plated their quesadillas and sat beside her at the bar. They ate in silence a few minutes. Bronwyn wasn't sure if it was the food or the comforting reassurance of his presence, but she felt a kind of warmth spreading through her midsection. They finished their food.

"I should go," she said, not wanting to leave.

"We could watch something," he suggested.

"Yes."

"Any suggestions?"

*"The West Wing."*

"Are you joking?" he asked.

"Yes," she said, scooting down off the high chair. "You choose because I don't care."

They went to the theater room and sat side by side on the couch. He turned to the Home and Garden channel and they watched a renovation show.

"Are you watching this for my benefit?" she asked.

"Nope," he replied.

"That house is only three hundred thousand?" she gasped. "It would go for close to two million here."

"Let me tell you about this mythical land called 'Middle America.' Legend has it the cost of living is affordable and, now brace yourself, they couldn't care less about politicians or their lives."

"Stop it, you're freaking me out," she said, shuddering.

He glanced at her then glanced back, his gaze lingering. "You know, you've got a lot of good raw material to work with."

She fanned her face. "It makes me so hot when guys talk about my raw material."

"I'm serious. You're pretty and..."

She held up a hand. "I'm pretty?"

"Has no one ever told you you're pretty before?"

"Does 'you'd be pretty if you lost fifteen pounds' count?" she asked.

"No. Geez, who said that to you?"

"My mom."

He closed his eyes and shook his head. "No, it doesn't count, it never counts. You are pretty, unequivocally pretty. You're funny and sweet and, presumably, reasonably intelligent. I don't get it. Why are you such a mess?"

"Because when it's like this, when I'm comfortable and relaxed, I feel okay. Everything seems to go fine. But I get within ten feet of my mom or anything related to my mom, and it all falls apart. I turn into a blithering, desperate, tongue-tied idiot. And, as my life would have it, everything is related to my mom. She chose my college, her alma mater. She picked my major, arranged my roommate and friends, and then got me the job post college, the one that ended today."

"Why don't you refuse her help and influence?" he asked.

"Because I can't. Because she scares me. Because she believes I can't do anything on my own. Because I think she's probably right."

"Want to hear something good?" he asked.

"Desperately."

"I am the furthest thing from your mom there is."

She regarded him as he regarded her. Then, smiling, she linked her arm with his. "Julian, I think this is the beginning of a beautiful friendship."

"That's good. Did you just make that up?"

"Absolutely," she said. "You don't watch a lot of old movies, do you?"

"Never."

"Good, let's keep it that way." She gave his arm a squeeze and they faced the TV again.

# CHAPTER 4

The next morning Bronwyn's reservations returned, and so did her despair. Last night after leaving Julian, who made her swear not to "off yourself badly" in his absence, she had chucked the razor blade in the trash. This morning she dug it out and set it on her nightstand. She wanted an out, in case things went south again.

She wasn't sure about the new friendship with Julian, but neither did she have any other options. In fact she had no options. She had been away from DC for an entire day and her phone hadn't buzzed once. No one cared if she lived or died, no one but the disenfranchised son of her mother's archrival. And she had the feeling his interest was more self-centered, to keep his mind preoccupied from whatever plagued it. Nonetheless, something broken was better than nothing at all. People dying in the desert didn't complain because the only water source had a bit of sand in it.

So she knocked on his back door bright and early. He answered, looking still groggy, wearing the same grungy clothes and bathrobe. "I wondered if you wanted to go into town and get scones," she said. Obviously they couldn't be seen in public together, but the local town was a bit of an anomaly, filled to the brim with rich and privileged politicians and therefore the rules need not apply.

"No, thanks," he said, his voice scratchy as if he'd just woken up.

To Bronwyn, overflowing with insecure vulnerability, it sounded like a rejection. "Oh, OK. Sorry." She turned to go. He grabbed her by the back of the pants and hailed her back.

"Yoo-hoo."

She turned around and looked down. He was holding out his foot for her inspection. She glanced at it and saw an ankle monitor on it, the kind for people who were on house arrest.

"Can't go out," he added.

She glanced behind him into the well-stocked gourmet kitchen. "I could make something."

"Omelets?" he asked, grinning.

"Only storybook men make those."

"What do storybook women do?" he asked, leaning on the door.

She pressed her palm to his cheek. "Watch and learn, baby."

The morning was a reverse of the night before. Julian sat on the high chair and watched while Bronwyn bustled around the kitchen, making a huge mess but also an amazing batch of blueberry scones.

"Where'd you learn to bake?" he asked.

"Fat camp," she said, and he laughed. "Not joking. We fatties have some amazing skills in the kitchen."

"Bronwyn, you are not fat," he said.

"On the inside, I am. Once a fat girl, always a fat girl."

"But you were never fat," he said.

"I was chubbier than my sisters. Than my brothers. Than our obese cat that ironically resembled Wilford Brimley and died from diabetes. I didn't fit the standard. My mom believed I lacked discipline and set out to change it."

"Your mom is a piece of work," he groused.

"Your mom's no saint," she snapped.

"No, but, not shockingly, my mom's laissez-faire parenting style ran the opposite gamut. Want to smoke pot in your bedroom at twelve? Let me make sure you have the good stuff. Want to host drunken parties with your friends at fourteen? Wouldn't want anyone to think I'm not the cool mom, so invite them all. Want to lose your virginity at fifteen to our twenty nine year old housekeeper? That's going too far because, say it with me, Bronwyn," he paused and Bronwyn recited it with him as if by rote, "good housekeepers are hard to find."

They polished off the scones. She made a second pot of coffee, and they moved back to the entertainment room, resuming the same spots they'd used the night before. "What's up with the bathrobe, Hef?"

"I'm convalescing," he said.

"Is convalescing man speak for losing touch with hygiene?" she asked.

"I guess I am due for a cleaning." He held up an armpit and sniffed, grimacing at the smell. "You know I knew Hugh Hefner. I went to the Playboy Mansion where I…"

She pressed her hands over her ears and shook her head. He plucked her hands away. "Got high, became unconscious, and had to be revived by his doctor. Shockingly, I was never invited back. My time there was brief, but it was…"

She pressed her hands back over her ears.

He plucked them away again. "Sad."

She dropped her hands. "Why sad?"

"Because the bunnies desperately wanted to be special, to be loved, to be *it*, and I couldn't take it. They were interchangeable, replaceable, disposable. You see, Bronwyn, I've always had this curse: I see through to the heart of people. I don't know if it's genetic or if it was something I picked up living with a career politician. But I can slice through layers of doublespeak like a hot machete through butter to see what's underneath and, depressingly, there's not a lot of good to be had in the world." He slunk down and rested his head on the back of the couch.

Bronwyn surprised them both by reaching over to pet his head. He reached out and rested his hand on her knee. "I have the opposite problem. I build people up in my mind, think they're better than they are. And then I'm perpetually disillusioned when I learn they're not."

"Let me save you some time with me: I'm a broken, messed up, wasted piece of humanity with little to no redeeming value," he said.

"I know," she agreed, and he laughed. She slunk down beside him and linked her arm with his. "What did you do?" she tapped the ankle monitor with her foot.

"Broke probation."

"What were you on probation for?" she asked.

"Drug possession with an intention to distribute."

"And you swung house arrest for that?" she said.

"I'm white, rich, and handsome. You do the math."

She snorted a laugh.

"What? You don't believe in white privilege?"

"No, I don't believe there's a judge dumb enough to believe you're not a flight risk. I mean, your parents own multiple houses and a private jet," she said.

"I don't wanna fly the coop. I just want to get it over with and have done with it. I'm almost there, the end is in sight, so long as I don't mess it up again," he said.

"How long have you been here?" she asked.

"Five months."

"Alone?"

"Minus the housekeeper and an occasional visit from a friend, yes."

"Wow, that's rough," she said.

"Eh, I had it coming."

She blinked at him in surprise.

"Ownership is one of the twelve steps," he said.

"Are you sober?" she asked.

"Eighteen months. The probation violation was because I had a friend in the car who had drugs on him."

"That seems unfair," she said.

"It was my fifth offense. I should have been in prison long ago. I'm not really complaining. Well, much. Plus it's been kind of nice to take some time away from life, to disappear for a while. Given me lots of time to think."

"What have you been thinking about?" she asked.

"Hypocrisy. I'm over it, done. And negativity. When this is over, I'm purging the bad people from my life, once and for all. From now on I'll be real, and I expect the same from the people around me. Or else."

"How far can you stray from home?"

"A few hundred feet," he said.

"Can you get it wet?"

"I get it, I need to shower. I'll put it on my agenda."

"It's supposed to be a scorcher today. Do you want to swim?" she asked.

"Are you inviting me to the sacred, hallowed halls of the Porter estate?"

"I believe I am," she replied.

"Swimming sounds exemplary," he said.

She whistled. "Prep school was not wasted on you."

"No, ma'am. I am all kinds of smart. That's why I excel at my career as a wastrel. You should hear the other hobos' vocabulary. Disgraceful."

Bronwyn laughed. "I think I've now joined your rank as hobo, seeing as I'm unemployed and homeless."

"Someone will snap you up in no time. What do you do?"

"I have no idea," Bronwyn said. "Perhaps if I'd ever actually learned my job title and responsibilities, I'd still be working there."

Julian laughed.

"I'm not kidding. I worked there for five years, and to this day I can't tell you what I did. I sort of showed up and went through the motions of inputting information, but I never had any idea what it was."

"What did you go to school for?"

"Business administration," she said.

"Bronwyn, I've known you for one day, and even I could tell you that's the wrong track for you. You should have been a preschool teacher or in some kind of service industry."

She sighed. "I know."

"What would you do if you could do anything? What was your dream when you were a little girl?" he prompted.

"I can't tell you, it's too embarrassing."

"I would have to check a calendar to see when I last bathed myself. Believe me when I tell you I have a high threshold for humiliation," he prompted.

She took a breath. "When I was little, I dreamed of nothing more than being a stay-at-home mom, the kind with a minivan who bakes cakes from scratch and throws killer birthday parties. I wanted to be married to the guy who would coach our kids' soccer team. I wanted to be in it together, the kind of unbreakable partners who can weather anything, the kind who make their kids feel indisputably loved and valued. And that's it, that's all. No career ambition, no drive to succeed. Nothing. Just a mom, a wife and a mom."

"That's not nothing. It's everything. I think you and I would each give anything to have a family like that. Think how different our lives would be if we had."

"My mom used to be like that. When I was *really* little, before she got elected. We were a normal, regular family. She stayed home with us while my dad went to work. And she baked and cleaned and shopped for groceries, took us to the park and the zoo. But it wasn't enough for her. *We* weren't enough for her. So she turned to politics and never looked back."

"And somewhere along the way, you got lost in the shuffle," he guessed.

She gave him a sad smile and a shrug.

"Why don't you do it?" he asked.

"Do what?"

"Why don't you find yourself some nice Midwestern boy, move to the boonies, have a million kids, and be the kind of woman you want to be?"

"I'm no expert on relationships, but I think when most men picture the future mother of their children, a jobless, homeless, insecure, suicidal failure doesn't spring to mind."

He put his arm around her, and she leaned on his shoulder.

"Do you think swimming counts as a shower?" he asked.

She sniffed him. "Definitely no."

"Right, then let's get to it. I've got a lot on my agenda today," he said.

"That *Real Housewives* marathon?" she guessed.

"Plus a *House Hunters* marathon. I'm double booked. Stressful."

She laughed, stood, and led the way to her house.

# CHAPTER 5

Once home, Bronwyn dithered in her bedroom for a while, inspecting herself in the mirror. She hadn't been swimming in ages. The only swimsuit in her possession was a two piece she bought after she lost fifteen pounds in college. She had regained five of those, making the suit uncomfortably tight on her upper half. Unfair as it was to struggle with weight, it was doubly unfair the first place she gained or lost it was her bust. The suit looked good on her, and that was a bad thing, in her mind. She didn't want it to seem like she was hitting on Julian because she wasn't. Not that it would matter if she were. He was notoriously gay, having come out sometime after college. Still, there were those women who fell for gay men, whether because they wanted someone safe or they wanted a challenge, Bronwyn had no idea. She had never been in that camp. Everyone she had ever crushed on had been decidedly straight, to the best of her knowledge. Therefore it had always been for personal reasons things had never worked out, reasons like her crippling insecurity and tendency to bumble into catastrophe. A man could only rescue a woman so many times before he grew weary of it. Bronwyn was too much for any man. Even Julian would eventually tire of her, she was sure. For now he was a literal prisoner of his house and therefore at her mercy. But once he was unleashed, once he could rejoin society and normal, functioning people, he would want nothing more to do with her.

"Bronwyn," he said, and she jumped about a foot.

"What are you doing here?" she said, spinning to look at him as he stood in the doorway of her room.

"You invited me."

"I invited you to swim, not to my bedroom. Give me a heart attack, why don't you," she pressed her hand to her heart, which was the wrong thing to do because it drew his attention there.

He glanced down and grinned. "Geez, you sure know how to fill out a bikini."

"It was the only suit at my disposal," she said, her hands fluttering nervously to her side. "Stop staring, You're literally leering at me, like you're practicing to be the creepy old guy in a bathrobe who goes to the park to flash people."

"Spoiler alert: you don't have to be old for that," he informed her, but he drew his eyes back up to meet hers and held out his hand. "Are you coming? What's the holdup?"

She decided to be honest. So far nothing she'd said had put him off, so why start trying to hide her crazy under a bushel? "I didn't want you to think I was coming on to you, you know, with the bikini and all." She took his hand and followed him outside.

He laughed. "Honey, if you were coming on to me, you wouldn't be wearing anything at all."

"Has that actually happened to you?" Her family wasn't merely politically conservative; they were morally and religiously conservative, too. In fact her mother hadn't approved of the two piece she was now wearing, despite the fact that Bronwyn had been legally an adult when she bought it. It was therefore unfathomable to her there were people in the world who skinny dipped or took off their clothes to throw themselves at strangers.

"Oh, Bronwyn, you're such a little lamb," Julian replied. They stopped by the edge of the pool. He took of his robe and set it aside before peeling down to his boxers.

"Are those going to stay on in the water?" she asked.

"I guess we'll find out," he said and jumped in. He surfaced and faced her. "Are you coming?"

"I don't like to jump in. I like to ease into it."

"I could have guessed that about you." He held out his arms to her. "Come on, Daddy will catch you."

"Please never call yourself 'Daddy' again in my presence," she said.

"Why? I thought you have Mommy issues."

"I have everything issues," Bronwyn said and then plugged her nose and jumped. Julian caught her and they went down before springing back to the surface. They swam for a long time, lap after lap after lap until, finally exhausted, they eased to the shallow end and sat on the steps.

"You're a good swimmer," Julian noted. "Were you on the swim team?"

"No. My mom thought I would miss too many campaign events."

"But I know for a fact your sisters and brothers played soccer, rugby, and lacrosse."

"Yes, but I got to go to fat camp, so it all balances out," Bronwyn said, and he laughed.

"The more you tell me about your family, the more I think you actually turned out pretty well, considering," he said.

"That may be the nicest thing anyone has ever said to me."

"Sad, so, so sad," he said. "I was thinking while I was swimming."

"And yet you didn't drown. You must be a skilled multitasker."

"Shh, Daddy's talking." She started to object, but he pressed his hand over her mouth. "Besides the soccer mom thing, what do you want most in the world?"

She thought for a long time before she spoke. "I guess I'd like to fit in the world I currently inhabit. I'd like to make my mom proud, to be part of her life and her work."

"That's what I thought you'd say."

"Are you going to talk me out of it? Is this the point you tell me my life should be more than trying to please my mom like we're in an afterschool special?"

"No, it's the point where I tell you I'm going to help you. Call me Professor, Eliza Doolittle. Your elocution lessons start today."

"I've already had elocution lessons," she informed him. "I used to say my r's funny."

"Okay, pet, you're being much too literal. I meant I'm going to turn you into one of them."

"Why?"

"Because it's what you want," he said.

"But…why?"

"Because I've spent thirty years living completely for myself; it's time to live for others."

"And your first altruistic act is to help me, a privileged white girl, fit into my uppercrust conservative family?"

"I'm starting small and working my way up. This week I help you with your millionaire parents. Next week I take a vow of poverty. Now, I'm going to go, wait for it, shower, and then I'll meet you back in my kitchen." He started to stand and paused. "PS. The boxers, not holding up so well. You've been warned." He took a step out of the pool, and she averted her eyes, shading them with her hand.

Julian laughed. "Such a little lamb," he muttered before jumping the hedge and heading home.

CHAPTER 6

Bronwyn took her own shower and went back to Julian's house, letting herself in without knocking. He sat at the computer in the kitchen.

"Great, you're here. Let's get started."

She came to stand behind him, peering over his shoulder. On the screen was her mother, along with everyone on her team. "Can I ask you a question before we get started?"

"Yes."

"No offense, but you're a self-avowed screw-up. How can you possibly help me?"

He used his foot to pull a chair beside him and patted it. She sat. "First of all, any time someone begins a sentence with, 'No offense,' rest assured they're about to say something offensive, so brace yourself. Now, to answer your question, merely because I don't partake in my mother's life does not mean I don't understand it. The same curse that enables me to see people's hearts also enables me to read their intentions, to understand complex social dynamics. But you raise an interesting and important point. What do you do when people insult you?"

"Cry."

"What if they say something mean but don't actually intend to hurt your feelings?"

"Cry."

"What if…"

She held up a hand to halt him. "I'm going to save you some time here, Julian. The answer to everything is cry. I'm a crier."

"Huh. Okay, not great, but I enjoy a challenge." He faced her and rested his hands on her thighs. "Listen to me, the problem isn't them; the problem is you."

She blinked at him. "As someone who grew up with a critical mother, I can assure you that harshly telling me the truth and disguising it as tough love does not work with me."

"You're not getting what I'm telling you. Who is the nicest person you know?"

"Louisa."

"Okay, so if Louisa snapped at you and called you stupid, what would you do?"

"I would be worried about her because I know how out of character that is."

"Good."

"I gave the right answer?" she asked, scooting forward slightly.

"You gave the perfect answer," he assured her, smoothing his palms on her legs. "The problem is on first contact you have no way of knowing who is like Louisa and who is like your mother; who is merely having a bad day and who is inherently evil." Her nose wrinkled at the description of her mother, but she didn't interrupt. "Thanks to your mom's brand of tender, loving care, you've been conditioned to believe everyone sees your faults, everyone is picking on you. What you need to learn to do is assume everyone is like Louisa, everyone has your best interest at heart but is merely having a bad day."

"But that's not always true," she interjected.

"See, it doesn't matter because, in either case, they're strangers who have nothing to do with your life. It doesn't matter if they don't like you. It doesn't matter if they hate you. It doesn't matter if they think you're the intellectual equivalent of tar paper."

"I get it, thanks."

"It's imperative you do because this is fundamental. You can't go around absorbing all the world's hurts. There are too many; it will destroy you. You have to learn to deflect. This is how you deflect, by telling yourself every single time it's not about you. That's the first thing I want you to practice. If someone says something to you that you perceive to be mean, I don't want you to picture your mother. I want you to picture Louisa, to convince yourself they're probably a wonderful person who is merely having a bad day you've had the misfortune to intercept."

"Julian." She took his hands in hers, clasping them. "I think you said in five minutes what my therapist didn't in five years."

"Did your mother pick your therapist?"

She nodded. "She also came with me to most of my sessions so they could compare notes on things we needed to work on."

He touched his fingers to her lips, hushing her. "Maybe don't tell me any more things like that, baby doll. We don't want me going John Hinckley, Jr. on your mother."

Beneath his fingers, her lips curled into a smile. He smiled in return and dropped his hand. "So, when you're in a social setting, I want you to pretend you're a ping pong paddle. Paddles are soft, but non-absorbent. They are made to bounce balls, to deflect and return. That's what you're going to do. If someone asks you a question, don't answer the question. Turn it into a better question and give it back to them. If someone hurls an accusation, laugh and say something quippy."

"I'm not good at quippy. Can I interest you in a complete mental breakdown? I'm aces at those."

"Let's practice: Bronwyn, we've recently uncovered unflattering pictures of you stuffing your face at fat camp. Care to comment?"

"Your mom," she said.

Julian scrubbed his face with his hand. "We'll come back to that, but, for the record, don't ever, ever say 'your mom' to a reporter. Also unacceptable would be anything that includes the phrase, 'I'm rubber, you're glue.'"

"Got it," she said.

"Now, let's talk about your appearance."

She frowned touching her fingertips tentatively to her hair.

"Don't give me that look," he said.

"What look?"

"Like you're bracing for a beating. I already told you you're pretty. That hasn't changed in the last twenty four hours. But your camp is conservative, and you're bohemian. You're more in line with us, looks wise. You need to be less Nancy Sinatra and more Nancy Reagan."

"Nancy Sinatra? Nancy Rea...How old are you?"

"In my heart I'm ancient." He motioned to her head. "The hair is too carefree, too wild."

"You don't like my hair?" Her big, crazy hair was the best part of her, her favorite feature. If she didn't have her hair, she had nothing.

Julian cupped her face in his hands. "I love your hair. I adore your hair. I would marry your hair tomorrow. But for the sake of what we're doing here, it needs to be tamed. Consider it a metaphor. Smooth it down and pin it up."

"Next you're going to tell me I have to start wearing pantsuits."

"Pantsuits are Hillary's thing; don't take that away from us," he said. He cocked his head, studying her. "Skip the suit, go retro sweet. Swing dresses with tapered waists, something feminine and innocent. The old codgers will eat that up and the women will think you look like a nonthreatening Audrey Hepburn which, by the way, you kind of do."

"You think Audrey Hepburn looks threatening?" she asked.

"You don't?" he countered, shuddering.

She laughed. He turned them to face the computer. "Let's go over personnel. Feel free to take notes, this is going to be a blitz of information."

She made no move to pick up the pen he'd set out for her. "I said take notes," he snapped, and she lunged for the pen and paper, holding them aloft.

"You're kind of a terrifying control freak," she said.

"Of course I am—I'm an only child. Let's start on the low end of the totem pole and work our way up to your mother."

Now it was her turn to shudder. He rested his hand on her leg and gave it a reassuring squeeze. "She can't hurt you here, it's only a picture."

"Would that that were true," she muttered and started taking notes.

After a supper they cooked together, they retired to the entertainment room again. As before, they sat together on the couch. Unlike before, he reached to a basket on the floor, picked up a ball of yarn, and started to knit.

"You knit," she observed stupidly.

"When I gave up smoking, I needed an outlet for my nervous fingers. Same principle as when I gave up drinking and drugging. Basically needlework has seamlessly taken the place of all my former vices, terrible pun intended."

"Knitting does all that?"

"Knitting, crochet, embroidery, and most recently quilting."

"Wow," she mouthed, half impressed and half amused. She had never known a man who did any of those things before, or at least not one who was willing to admit it. "Can I ask you a question?"

"I'd say 'shoot,' but, given your family's affinity for guns and close affiliation with the NRA, I'm afraid you'd take me literally. So go ahead."

"Do you have a significant other?"

He squinted. "I understand the words, but not the odd inflection you've given them. What are you getting at?"

"Do you, um, have a…boyfriend?"

He lowered the knitting and looked at her. "You think I'm gay?"

"Don't you think you're gay?" she countered.

"No, in fact I'm certain I'm not. Haven't you ever known a straight guy who knits?"

"No, actually, but it's not the knitting. It's *People* magazine."

"What does *People* have to do with my knitting?" he asked.

"There was an article stating you were gay," she said.

"You grew up in a political family, and you believe things you read in the press?" he said, incredulous.

"There was also a picture of you at a Pride parade."

"So? One of my best friends is gay. He asked me to go and I have this weird quirk where I support my friends and show up when they ask me to appear."

"So…" she drawled. "The picture plus the article plus any lack of denial from your mom's camp equals woman who believed you were gay until about thirty seconds ago."

"I kissed you," he reminded her. "All those years ago. The memory's a little hazy, thanks, cocaine, but I'm pretty sure it was a good, solid kiss."

"Maybe I turned you," she said and he sputtered a laugh. "Seems like something I would do."

"Let me set your mind at ease: I am not, nor have I ever been, gay."

"Why didn't you say that when the magazine said you were?"

"One, because I didn't care. The people closest to me know the truth. Two, because my mom loved it. It really helped her with the Alphabets."

"The Alphabets?"

"LGBTQA crowd."

"Are you allowed to call them the Alphabets? I thought that was derogatory."

"Only when your camp does it. They're our constituents; we can call them anything we want."

"Oh." She picked up the end of his afghan, inspecting it.

"What?" he asked.

"Nothing."

"Don't do the girl thing. Spit it out."

"We've spent a lot of time together the last few days, close contact, swimming, touching."

"And…"

"And I thought it was fine because I thought you were gay."

"Now that you know I'm not, it's not fine?" he asked.

"No, it's still fine, but I thought you weren't attracted to me because you weren't attracted to any women. And now I learn you're not attracted to me because you're not attracted to me."

He paused, sighing. "Bronwyn, do you want me to be attracted to you?"

"Theoretically, no. In reality, a little temptation would be nice."

"You're very tempting," he said patronizingly, patting her head.

"Wow, my self-confidence bucket is bursting now. Feels good, thanks."

"If your self-esteem comes from a man, it's coming from the wrong place," he said.

"You sound like every counselor, priest, and fellow elevator passenger I've ever encountered," she said, and he laughed. "Can you teach me to knit?"

"Probably not. But I'll give it a go." He leaned closer and began explaining what he was doing. As predicted, Bronwyn didn't get it at all, but she enjoyed the opportunity to try.

# CHAPTER 7

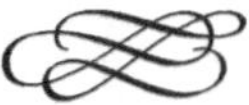

The next morning, Bronwyn let herself into Julian's house, walked into the living room, and came face to face with Carlo Garcia, Louisa's son, her crush since she was seventeen years old.

"Carlo," she blurted.

He turned to face her with a broad smile, one that had only grown more handsome and distinguished with the passing years. "Bronwyn. I have never seen you here before."

"Carlo, hi," she repeated. She was staring at him, blinking rapidly as if she were having a seizure. "Hi, Carlo."

"Oh, geez," Julian muttered, and that was when Bronwyn comprehended he was also in the room.

She also realized, suddenly, how odd it must seem to Carlo for her to be there, knowing how separate their families were. She cast about for the first explanation she could find. Unfortunately, it was a horrible one. "I came to borrow..." her eyes scanned the room and landed on the couch. "This pillow." She held the pillow aloft.

Carlo's smile wavered, his eyes now looking confused.

"Okay, that's enough of that." Julian grabbed her by the scruff of the neck and hauled her toward the kitchen like a mangy stray. "Make yourself at home, Carlo. Back in a minute." He dragged Bronwyn to the back door and let her go. "What was that?"

"I don't know," she said, covering her face with her hands.

"Have you ever encountered the male of the species before?"

"Yes, but he's so dreamy; I get flustered. The good news is I found a new method and I'm going to go suffocate myself with this pillow." She held the pillow aloft again.

Julian took the pillow out of her hands and tossed it away. "First, you're twenty seven years old. Never say 'dreamy' again unless you're using it ironically. Here, I'll demonstrate: Your performance in there was *dreamy*. Now go away and don't have contact with him again until I fix you. I mean it, not a peep, not a showing, not a hello. You are seriously not ready."

"I know, I know, you're right."

"Good, now go away, you disgust me." He kissed her forehead, opened the door, and shoved her through.

Bronwyn opened the door and stuffed her head back inside. "When you say 'fix' you don't mean that literally, right? Like, you're not going to neuter me?"

"We'll talk," he hissed and closed the door in her face.

Left to her own devices, Bronwyn wandered back to her house and meandered through. She had purposely avoided doing so since she'd been back, not wanting to see a visual of her family dysfunction played out in pictures. Now she stood at the mantel and studied the faces of her siblings—Scott, Lena, Edward, Katelyn, and Phillip. Five siblings, and she wasn't close to one of them. She was the consummate middle child, ignored, forgotten, overlooked, fourth in line to the throne. Her brothers and sisters had all distinguished themselves with their beauty, their talents, their intelligence, their accomplishments, their obsequious manners. And then there was Bronwyn. Not even her height had cooperated. Somehow the gene that made everyone else in her family tall and lithe had mutated, leaving her five foot three and curvaceous. There were pictures of all of them on the mantel—in lacrosse uniforms, soccer uniforms, baseball uniforms.

Three of her siblings had gone into the military, and those uniform pictures had been added to the mix.

There was one picture of Bronwyn, possibly the most unfortunate year of her life when she was fifteen, chubby, sporting braces, glasses and a sunburn. As if it could get any worse, the terrible sunburn only covered one third of her because she fell asleep by the pool with a book on her face. More painful than that tragic remembrance of adolescence were the family pictures. Despite the fact that Bronwyn had two younger siblings, she somehow ended up on the end of every lineup. Every single one, off by herself to the side, slightly askew from the family pose. She could only be more of an outcast if she wore leper's sackcloth and a sign proclaiming herself unclean.

"Oh, Miss Bronwyn," Louisa exclaimed from behind her, her accent as heavy as it had been for as long as Bronwyn could remember.

"Louisa," Bronwyn exclaimed, hurrying forward to throw her arms around the woman who hugged her tightly in return. "How have you been?"

"I am good, very good. But how is my pretty girl?" Louisa cupped Bronwyn's cheek, and she remembered what she told Julian was untrue. Louisa had always called her pretty. How could Bronwyn have forgotten?

"I'm…" Bronwyn started and then stopped, not sure how to continue. She had been about to reply she was good, but she wasn't. The razor blade still on her nightstand was a testament to that. She was homeless and jobless, basically a complete loser in all the ways that mattered. "I'm…" She cast about for something positive to say. "I'm alive."

"In the end, that's all any of us can say, *niñita*. Eh, your parents aren't due back for some time, so I didn't go to the market. Should I add some food for you? Will you be here long?"

"Yes, please. But no rush. I've been eating with a friend."

"Ah, it sounds like my little one has a boyfriend, yes?"

"No, just a friend."

"Ah." She eyed Bronwyn with what could only be calculation. "Carlo is next door, I'll tell him to come say hello, yes?"

"No," Bronwyn blurted. After her failed attempt already this morning under Julian's watchful eye, she could only imagine the damage she could do on her own. She'd likely end up setting something on fire.

"Oh," Louisa said, her soft eyes turning to hurt.

Bronwyn grasped her hand. "I already saw him. At Julian's. I said hello there, and I would hate to disturb him again. Carlo is looking, uh, well." He was looking beautiful, as always.

Louisa blinked at her. "You were at the Baxter's? Did we have their mail by mistake?"

"No. Julian and I are...friends."

Louisa's eyes widened with either horror or fear. Maybe both. She put her hand to her mouth and shook her head. "No, *chica*, no. Your mother." She froze and looked around as if expecting Laurel Porter to show up suddenly, as if she'd been conjured. Knowing her mother as she did, it was a reasonable fear.

"Mom's on the campaign trail, Louisa. She'll never know. It will be okay, I promise. Besides, Julian's okay."

Louisa nodded her assent. "Julian and Carlo are friends from boyhood days, but it's different with you."

"It always has been," Bronwyn agreed tiredly.

Louisa squeezed her hand. "Be careful, little one. Please."

"I will," Bronwyn promised, returning the squeeze.

She puttered while Louisa worked, ghosting through the vast house like a stranger, checking every room for some hidden sign she somehow fit. When she found none, she returned to the living room and stared at the mantel.

"That is one bad picture of you," Julian remarked, coming to stand beside her.

"The worst. My senior picture was actually good. I was having a good hair day, and the braces and glasses were gone by then, along with the puffy-faced sunburn. But this is the one we keep to show visitors."

Julian put his arm around her and turned her away from the mantel. "We have a wrinkle."

Bronwyn looked down, inspecting her t-shirt. He put his finger under her chin and tipped it back up. "A figurative wrinkle," he clarified.

"What's that?"

"I was talking to Carlo."

She gripped his biceps. "Did he mention me?"

"Yes, he asked if you'd recently suffered a stroke that made you blink a lot and forget how to talk like regular people," he said. "He said my mom's been in contact. She wants him."

Bronwyn grimaced. "She's more than twice his age. And married."

He put his hands on her shoulders and gave her a little shake. "I would pay money to see inside your head. She wants him for her campaign; she wants his vote."

"Why?"

"Because he's the immigrant son of your mother's housekeeper. If she secured his vote, it would tie up the Latinx swing vote for certain. That means your mom is going to want him."

"And that's bad?"

"No, baby, that's good. What we have here is a two birds with one stone situation. You tie up Carlo, you get in your mom's good graces."

"I told you I'm bad with knots," she said.

"I didn't mean…" he began and realized she was joking. "Oh. That was an unexpectedly naughty double entendre. Kudos."

"Don't you mean knotty?" she returned, elbowing him. "Huh, huh?"

"Okay, you ruined it, along with the chances of any man ever finding you sexy."

"It was always a long shot." Her phone buzzed with a text, and she froze.

"Your mom?" he guessed.

"How did you know?"

"Because you're wearing the same expression I wore last time I was in jail and got cornered by a guy named Big Chunk." He watched as she read the text, her face falling with undisguised hurt and pain. "What did she say?"

She held the phone aloft and read out loud. "The police found your things scattered in a hallway and wanted me to check you're not dead." She glanced up at him. "Heartwarming, isn't it? The Mother's Day card practically writes itself."

He reached for the phone, texted a reply, and hit send.

"What did you say?" she asked, the sad set of her features slipping into a smile of anticipation.

He read out loud. "Having a tawdry affair with a prisoner. Will text again when it ends. Expect a long wait—he's lonely and desperate for loving."

She laughed. The phone buzzed again and she braced herself before reading aloud again. "Clean it up. The optics are bad."

"She's talking about your possessions in the hallway, isn't she?" he guessed.

"Yep. I don't think she believes I would ever do anything on my own, find someone myself without her direct involvement."

"But you did," he said, resting his hand on her knee. He gave it a squeeze. "Bronwyn Porter, I think it's time we showed your mother exactly what you're made of."

"That sounds great, Julian. Quick question: what am I made of?"

CHAPTER 8

Bronwyn arrived at Julian's early the next morning. She expected him to be once again in his bathrobe, but he was clean, shaved, dressed and, dare she admit, quite handsome.

"Let's shop," he said, glancing up at her with a smile of welcome when she remained frozen in the doorway, surprised by his sudden appeal.

"Have you been watching the Home Shopping Network again?" she asked.

"I bought a nonstick skillet that's going to change your life. But today we're going to buy clothes. It's time for your makeover, Eliza."

"Are you calling me that in the hopes I'll call you 'Professor'?"

"No. Teacher or Sir are equally hot," he said. "Come over here." He beckoned her toward where he sat at the desk. When she reached him, he pulled her into his lap and faced the computer. "I found some things, but I didn't know your size. The curves make it tricky." As if to demonstrate, he ran his hand from her hip to her waist and back again.

"Hmm, I…yes."

"It's good news for you, though. Carlo likes curves."

"Carlo?" she said. Who was Carlo? Sitting in his lap with his hands on her, she couldn't think past him.

"Carlo, the dreamy guy you stuttered at in this very spot yesterday," he reminded her. He gave her neck a squeeze as if to jolt her memory, but he had to slide his hand under her long hair to do so and the effect was ruined.

"Huh?"

"You are not awake this morning. Carlo." He clicked the computer and Carlo's bio came to life on the screen, along with his picture.

"Yowza," she said, suddenly remembering Carlo with crystal clarity. "Do you think he's prettier in person or in this picture?"

"In person," Julian said, and she turned to look at him. "What? He's a handsome man. Haven't you ever heard a straight man say that about another man? It happens a lot on my side of the aisle."

"On my side of the aisle straight men show their appreciation for each other by shooting things."

"So an animal has to die every time a bro wants to bond?" he asked, grimacing.

"First of all, we don't say bro. That's all on you guys. Second, you don't have to kill something every time you shoot a gun. Target shooting is good sport, or so my brothers, sisters, parents, grandparents, and cousins would have me believe."

"Not you?"

She sighed. "Guns make me nervous."

He laughed. "And I actually enjoy shooting. Maybe we were switched at birth."

"We should trade places, see if anyone notices," she suggested.

"Good idea. You wear the ankle monitor for a while." As if talking about it reminded him of his discomfort, he reached down and itched behind it.

"What happens after it comes off?" she asked.

"I go to my favorite restaurant to celebrate," he said.

"No, I mean after after. Will you go back to your job?"

"The word 'back' implies I ever had a job in the first place."

"You've never had a job?" she asked, aghast.

He shook his head.

"What will you do?" she asked.

"What I've always done: languish in style."

She blinked at him. "I don't understand. If you don't work, how do you get money?"

"I'm the only child of an only child whose father was a billionaire. You do the math. No, I mean I would like you to actually do the math and tell me how much is in my trust fund because I have no idea. But it's definitely enough to allow me to be a super rich hobo for the rest of my life."

"But what about your sense of purpose?"

"My sense of purpose is in being a decent human being," he said.

"What about contributing to society?"

"How does me working contribute to society?" he asked.

"Because you're being responsible, creating product, earning money, generating interest."

"That's not contributing to society; that's contributing to capitalism."

"But it's capitalism that allowed your grandfather to become a billionaire in the first place," she pointed out.

He shrugged. "My life is a vicious cycle of hypocrisy. I told you that already. My billionaire mother, who has also never worked a day in her life outside of politics, is the mouthpiece for the blue-collar working class, who ostensibly work a hundred hours a week and still barely make a living wage. And I used to rage against that, but my rage got me nowhere. So I've come to terms with it, and the peace I've found doesn't make me want to dull my emotions with illicit substances."

"It's really not fair," Bronwyn said.

"Which part?"

"All of it. Meanwhile my parents, who both came from decidedly working class roots, put themselves through college by working multiple jobs and lived on next to nothing when I was a kid. We had six kids, and my dad supported us all while my mom stayed home. Our clothes and Christmas presents came from Goodwill. It was that frustration with the disparity, with the system, that drove my mom into politics. She is undoubtedly the strongest woman I know, she ran a shoestring campaign, and unseated an incumbent, and yet people say our side oppresses women. And my parents are the ones who are branded as being out of touch with the working class, as being rich, old white snobs."

"They are rich, old white snobs," he pointed out.

"They are now, but they weren't always. They've only come into money since my mom became a politician." She paused, squinting as the statement registered. "It's all so messed up."

"Yes, yes it is," Julian agreed, giving her a squeeze. "Welcome to the Dark Side, baby girl. Your side has a narrative, and my side has a narrative, and none of the people leading both sides believe anything they say."

"How do we fix it?"

"Listen to you. So cute, so nubile. I've chosen to opt out in a big way. My mother doesn't even ask me to show up at events anymore. I lead my own life, separate from hers, and I don't touch politics with a ten-foot pole. My heart is too sensitive to see the glut of filth and lies up close, and so I don't. I turn a blind eye, go on about my business, and let the wolves devour each other. You, my precious, will have to come to your own conclusions about it. If you think you can fix it, then by all means try. But if you realize you can't, then get out quick before it kills you."

Sometime during the conversation she shifted sideways and rested her head on his chest. Both his arms were around her, his right hand smoothing her neck with his fingers. They sat in comfortable silence a few minutes before she spoke again. "It's not that I want to be in politics. I don't. You think I'm innocent, but I'm not. I've seen enough to last a lifetime, and I want no part of it. I just want..." she trailed off, unable to say the pathetic words out loud.

"You want your mom's approval."

She nodded against his chest.

"Who doesn't?" he said.

"Does your mom approve of you?"

"I'm a drug-addicted, alcoholic felon. But yes. Does she wish I were the political scion of her dreams? Absolutely. Has she made peace with the fact that I'm not? Yes."

"That must be phenomenal."

"It is. You have to love people where they are. It's the only way. My mom and I had our bumps when I was growing up—the aforementioned lack of boundaries chief among them. But she learned her lessons, and she never stopped loving me, never gave up on me when I was at my worst. That meant something. That meant everything. It was that love that was my lifeline when I was at my lowest."

"I think you might be my lifeline," she whispered. "And the saddest part is you're a stranger."

"I'm not a stranger," he replied, his hand making a soothing circle on her back. "I'm your neighbor. It's biblical for us to love each other."

"Technically you're my enemy," she pointed out.

"Still biblical." They remained lost in quiet thought a few minutes until he snapped to attention. "Are you ready to begin?"

"Teach me, Professor," she said, sitting up away from him.

"So hot," he whispered and clicked the computer to life.

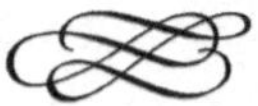

# CHAPTER 9

They spent the morning shopping, pausing only when Bronwyn pointed out she had no job and therefore no money for clothes.

"Your parents are loaded," Julian pointed out.

"Yes, my *parents* are loaded. They believe each of us needs to make our own way. It builds character."

"I don't believe that, and I have character coming out my ears. Therefore I'll pay for everything."

"I can't let you do that," she said.

"Why not?"

"Because part of being a responsible adult means not taking charity from others," she said.

He rubbed at a spot between his eyebrows. "I'm beginning to see why our two sides can't come to an agreement. Let me try it this way: this is my home and my castle, therefore I'm its king and you do what I say. I'm buying the clothes, and you will accept them with a smile."

"This is further proof socialists always become despots, but whatever because that dress is really, really pretty."

"Capitalists are always swayed by their greed, but you're going to look amazing so I'm buying the shoes, too."

After a full morning of shopping, they had lunch delivered from Julian's favorite restaurant.

"Let's have a conversation," Julian said when the food was finished.

"Is that not what we've been doing all morning?" she asked.

"A conversation with purpose, a discourse, if you will, on Bronwyn."

Sighing, she took a piece of paper and pen, prepared to write "Tell me what's wrong with me."

"It's easier if I write it down for you." He took the pen and spent a long time moving over the paper. When he handed it back, it had the word, "NOTHING," followed by a detailed picture of a whale and dolphin frolicking in the sea.

"It didn't take long to write, so I drew you a picture," he said.

"I don't understand," she said.

He pointed to the paper. "See, the whale and dolphin are friends. It's one of those plankton-eating whales."

"No, I mean I don't understand your list."

He pushed aside the paper and took her hands in his. "Bronwyn, seemingly from birth, your mother has tried to fit you into the box she had designed for you. Time after time after time after time she has shoved you in the box. As if that's not problematic enough, you've taken your inability to fit inside the box personally, as if it's some kind of defect you don't fit a mold not designed for you. You perceive these as a series of failures, when in reality they are a series of triumphs. No matter how hard she's tried, she hasn't been able to crush your spirit. It's indomitable, perseverant, unbreakable."

"Thank you, Roget, but I'm not sure I understand what you're getting at."

"Instead of continuing to try to be who she wants you to be, let's work instead on using who you already are."

She stared hard at the table, absently demolishing a napkin between her fingers. "What if who I am isn't enough?" she whispered.

He pulled the napkin out of her fingers and resumed his hold of her hands. When he didn't immediately reply, she finally drew her eyes up to meet his. "You are more than enough," he said with such quiet authority she began to believe him, at least a little.

"Does that go for Carlo, too?"

"Oh, no, child. You're a hot mess with men. Forget everything you've ever known."

"Done."

"Good. And now we begin to rebuild you."

"Can you make me bionic?" she asked.

"Baby, when I'm done with you, you'll be better than bionic. You'll be Bronwyn Porter."

"I'm already Bronwyn Porter."

"Exactly."

"Julian, I'm mourning the lost part of my childhood that didn't hang out with you sooner," she said.

"What a coincidence—I'm mourning the lost part of my childhood I can't remember because of all the drugs I took."

He sounded sincere and a little bit sad. She brought his hand to her lips and kissed his palm. "Think of all the years of memories ahead of you that are still to come."

He pressed the same palm to her cheek. "I am." After a few beats of staring at each other over the table, he once again snapped to attention. "Let's talk about men. For you, not me."

"If you say so."

He grabbed her around the waist and tilted her sideways over his lap. "What do I have to do to convince you I'm straight?"

She stared up at him, as handsome and charming as she remembered when he kissed her at sixteen. "Absolutely nothing." A little hum of tension buzzed between them. Bronwyn reached out a hand to caress his hair. Julian smiled, a slow little half smile that said he knew exactly what she was thinking. If so, she wished he would clue her in. A few hours ago she'd been sure she wanted Carlo, and now she wasn't so certain. Her fingers slid to his lips. He kissed them.

"Señor Julian," the housekeeper called, letting herself in the back door. She stopped short at the sight of them. "Oh."

"Hello, Lucia," Julian replied. He helped Bronwyn sit upright and let her go.

"Hello. I will start upstairs today," Lucia said, her startled gaze darting furiously to Bronwyn and back again. Bronwyn guessed Louisa would be getting an earful of conversation soon. The two longtime housekeepers had been friends for years. It would be interesting sometime to hear them compare notes.

"Where were we?" Bronwyn asked, straightening her shirt.

"We were discussing your irresistibility to mankind," Julian said. "And then you gave me a demonstration."

She laughed and the tension was dispelled.

Later they sat on his couch in what had become their usual positions. He was knitting something while Bronwyn watched TV. "Look at that girl," she said, her unblinking gaze fastened on the television. "I'd kill to have a body like that."

Julian reached out and took her hand. She thought he was giving it a reassuring kiss, but instead he brought it to his mouth and bit it. Hard.

"Ouch," she said, "You bit me."

"Cute and perceptive. That's a killer combo," he said.

"I think you drew blood," she said, inspecting her hand.

"Good. I'm going to keep biting you as long as you persist in the self-deprecating sad sack routine."

"I'll bleed out," she exclaimed.

"Or you'll stop." He lowered his knitting in frustration. "Bronwyn, do you know what men want?"

"Clearly not."

"Confidence."

"If I looked like that, I would be confident," she said.

"That's it." He tossed aside the knitting and leapt for her. She yelped and attempted to dart away from him, but he easily caught her. They struggled for a while, but eventually he pinned her, trapping her beneath him with her arms over her head. "Do you think that girl doesn't have problems? Do you think her breath doesn't stink?"

"I've never considered her breath," Bronwyn said.

"Don't play dumb."

"It's not an act."

He bit the tender underside of her arm.

"*Ouch,*" she said. "That one was a joke."

"You say stuff so often it's hard to distinguish." He kissed the place he'd bitten and released her. They sat up and he clasped her hand. "Bronwyn, seriously, you need to stop. If you want your life to change, then you have to change it. I get it, your mom messed you up bad with all the criticism and negative talk. Her voice has become your inner voice. But take it from someone who's had years of drug and alcohol abuse counseling—you can change your inner voice. I used to believe there was no way I could ever break the hold drugs and alcohol had on me, but I did it, one painful second at a time. This is your addiction, this negative self talk. It's okay if you don't feel confident right now, but you need to stop blurting your perceived deficiencies."

"I will try, genuinely I will. But I'm not very good at..." she stopped short and gave him a sheepish smile. "I'll try. There's one little problem, though."

"What's that?" he asked, reaching for his knitting again.

"I kind of like it when you bite me."

He laughed. "Maybe I'll do it for fun sometimes."

Bronwyn didn't comment, but she could have told him fun wasn't the feeling she got when he bit her. But as she didn't know what the feeling was, she let it go and didn't bring it up again.

# CHAPTER 10

"And breathe, and stretch. Stretch. Breathe."

"Yoga is exhausting," Bronwyn noted, yawning.

"It is," Julian agreed. "Imagine how much more exhausting it would be if we were actually doing it."

They lay side by side on the floor, a yoga workout streaming on the oversized television.

"What should we do tonight?" Bronwyn asked.

"We're exercising," Julian noted, draping his arm over her waist.

"I meant after, obviously," Bronwyn said, nestling close, snuggling her back to his front. "Fitness is important."

"I don't know," Julian said, his tone filled with uncharacteristic blasé.

Bronwyn rolled to face him. "What's wrong?"

"Nothing."

She poked him.

"Occasionally a bit of ennui sets in. It hasn't happened since you arrived because you're a clever distraction." He brushed the hair off her face, smiling. "But I've been in this house a long time. Every once in a while I want to break free."

"Oh." She sat up, her face alight with a new thought.

"What?" Julian asked, lying on the floor and gazing up at her.

"I've got it."

"The Golden Ticket? Shingles? What?" His hand reached out to twine in one of her curls, but she sat on his stomach and pinned his arms, beaming.

"I know what we can do," she said.

"I'm beginning to have some thoughts as well," he said, clasping her hands as they pressed his into the carpet.

"It's going to take some time to get everything ready," she said.

"I'm ready now," he said.

"No, it's going to be great, you'll see. I'll text you when it's time to come over." She kissed his cheek and rolled away, darting for the exit as Julian stared after her, smiling. He was no longer bored, and with Bronwyn it was a guarantee he couldn't remain so for long. She took joy in simple pleasures. Last night she had been ecstatic because an onion ring made it into her fry order by accident. She had set it aside, calling it the ring to rule all onion rings, her precious.

When he received her text sometime later, he realized he had fallen asleep. He stood, rifled his hands through his hair, and set off on the short walk to her yard. Stepping over the dividing hedge, he saw a row of twinkling fairy lights and a roaring outdoor fire.

"What's this?" he asked.

"Camping," she said, indicating the tent behind her with a flourish.

"Camping," Julian repeated, his tone dubious. "I was afraid my brawn would fool you into believing I'm a rugged outdoorsman, and now it's happened."

"You're going to love it, I promise," she said.

He was doubtful, but she looked so hopeful, so excited. "What does one do while camping?"

"When my family used to camp, we fished and cooked our food over a campfire."

His gaze darted to the river. Both their families had docks and boats, for that matter, but for his family it was more a status symbol, something for his parents to pull out on Memorial Day for a few hours. They'd never fished from it, and certainly never eaten what they caught.

"Fishing," he said, trying to sound enthused.

"Fishing the Bronwyn and Julian way," she said, revealing two takeout containers from their favorite local café. "Salmon for you, trout for me."

"Is the fire for ambiance?" he asked.

"The fire is for s'mores."

"Those melty things little kids eat?" he asked.

"There's no age limit on s'more love, Julian," she said seriously, handing him a bottle of water and his takeout container of fish.

"Is this what your family did all those nights out here?" he asked. When they were little, her family had seemingly spent the entire summer outdoors. Julian used to watch them sometimes, full of disdain for their lack of class. They had always been loud, barefoot, usually covered in water or grime. Unlike his family, hers had made good use of their river access, jumping off the dock and swimming in the dingy Potomac. When he was a kid, he'd considered them a bunch of toothless hillbilly rednecks, giving Bronwyn a pass because she had seemed like the lone outlier. But as he matured and mellowed, he began to see they were different than he was, not because of their political ideology but because there were so many of them. Laurel and her husband had likely sent them outside for some peace and quiet and, being a large group of adventurous children, they'd made their fun however they could.

"We loved to camp," Bronwyn confirmed. "When I was really little, we used to go to this cabin in the backwoods of Kentucky." She paused and glanced at him.

"What?"

"I was waiting for you to add a derisive comment about us being backwoods hillbillies," she said.

"What? No way." In truth, he probably would have except she sounded so wistful and nostalgic. Camping memories were obviously tender for her, too tender for him to poke at. "What was your favorite thing about camping?"

She chewed her bite of trout while she thought of her answer. "For that short time when we were camping, it felt like we were all equal. No one was better at camping."

She took another bite and now it was Julian's turn to chew thoughtfully. He had spent his life being *other* because he was an only child. She had spent her life being *other* because she felt less than everyone in her family. Maybe that was why they fit so naturally together; at last their otherness had found an affinity.

They finished their food and Bronwyn showed him how to make s'mores.

"I feel so blue collar," Julian said, licking melted chocolate from his fingers.

"Now when people accuse your mom of losing touch with the middle class, she can trot you out and show them your fingers that have touched flaming marshmallows." Bronwyn said.

"Flaming marshmallows sounds like a gay nightclub act," Julian said, reaching for the box of graham crackers.

Bronwyn laughed and he smiled. She was one of those people whose entire face lit when she laughed or smiled. The last few days she'd been doing both often, stark contrast to the state she was in when she first arrived. But what would happen when she submerged herself back within her mother's reach?

"Bronwyn, maybe we should cancel the plan," he blurted

"Cancel? Why?" She gazed at him with her too-big brown eyes, a smudge of chocolate on her nose, a glob of melted marshmallow on her chin. Julian felt like he'd made a massive mistake, as if he was sending her to certain doom.

"Because," he said.

"Because why, Julian?"

"We have a good thing going here, don't we? In our little cocoon, in our little corner of the universe?" He reached for a napkin and tried to clean her face but the napkin tore and stuck, making it appear as if she'd suffered a series of chocolate-related shaving mishaps.

"Yes, we have a good thing going, the best. Meeting you has been better than all the years of therapy combined and more fun than anything ever."

She was still oblivious to the food on her face, oblivious to the frayed pieces of napkin, oblivious to everything. Julian doused the tail of his shirt in water from his bottle and pulled it up to wash her nose and chin.

"So don't go. Don't ruin it. We'll go on as we've been. You and me, best pals, having fun day after day, healing all our broken pieces."

He finished bathing her face and dropped his shirt. She slid her arms around his neck and rested her head on his shoulder. He tipped his head, resting it on hers. "Julian, that's the most tempting offer I've ever had. But this little bit of heaven we've achieved is an illusion, it can't last."

"Why can't it?" he demanded, his hand making smooth passes up and down her spine. She was responsive to touch, ridiculously so, and melted into him, releasing whatever stress her body had been holding.

"Because it can't. You're here because of a punishment; I'm self-banished. Eventually your monitor is going to come off and you'll be free, but how will I ever be free?" she pulled back to look at him, searching his face for answers. "It's time for me to face the things I've been running away from my whole life; it's time for me to face my mother. Thanks to you, I feel ready to do that now. Unless...unless this is your way of telling me I'm not ready?"

How could he explain how much he hurt when she hurt? He smoothed his hands over her cheeks, smiling. "Sweet, it's in the bag. But, being a selfish creature by nature, it's all about me as usual. You're about to venture outside our magical realms of no responsibility and no outsiders. I'm going to miss you."

"Maybe I could put it off a little longer," Bronwyn said, now sounding uncertain.

Julian wanted to kick himself for instilling insecurity when he was supposed to be helping her grow stronger. "No, ignore me. Now is the time, and you're ready. You're so ready, B." She smiled and rested her head on his shoulder, snuggling close. "So what else do you crazy conservatives do on a campout?"

"First we crank country music," she said, and he groaned. "Then we get in our pickup trucks."

His answering groan grew louder.

"We head down to the Piggly Wiggly and buy some fireworks, something big, loud, and illegal."

"You're making that up," he accused.

"We have to be careful, though, a lesson we all learned well from Cousin Stumpy," she continued undaunted.

He tossed her over his shoulder and spun her around until she was laughing too hard to talk; it didn't take long. When he set her down, they crawled into the tent she'd assembled and watched a movie.

"I don't think we'll pass muster as hardy outdoorsmen," Bronwyn noted, reaching over to adjust the volume on Julian's iPad.

"We are totally roughing it; this screen is only eight inches," Julian said. He draped his arm over her, urging her closer. She complied, cuddling close and readjusting the blankets. "This redneck evening has been a lot of fun. Thanks for helping with my ennui."

"You're welcome, but rednecks don't say ennui," she said, smoothing the floppish hair off his forehead.

"What's the hillbilly way of saying I'm having fun with my favorite?" he asked.

"You say, 'Girl, if you were a chicken, you'd be impeccable.'"

He wasn't going to laugh, but he couldn't help it. And after the first sputter, he was lost, and so was Bronwyn. Eventually they gave up on the movie and spent the rest of the night trotting out their worst and most ridiculous pickup lines. She would be tired tomorrow, but the night of laughter with Julian was worth it. Soon she'd be back in her mother's world, and all laughter would come to a grinding halt.

# CHAPTER 11

Bronwyn didn't look in the mirror. She was afraid she wouldn't like what she saw. Instead she went to see Julian, hoping his eyes would tell her what she wanted to know.

He was asleep on the couch when she let herself in. She knelt beside him and touched his arm. He opened his eyes and blinked at her, confused. "Are you real?"

"I try to be," she said.

"You must be real. Dream Bronwyn wouldn't say that." He sat up. "You look perfect, beautiful, incredible."

"Did you actually have a hand in writing the thesaurus?" she asked, but she was blushing. "Thank you."

"Haven't you seen you?" he asked.

She shook her head. "Clearly I had to when I did my hair and makeup because not looking when you do those doesn't end well, but I didn't dwell, and I haven't seen the final product with the dress and everything. I didn't want to know if it didn't turn out well."

"It turned out well. It turned out amazing, indescribable, astonishing."

She laughed. He pulled her into his lap and put his arms around her. "I wish you were coming with me." She rested her head on his shoulder.

"You're going to do great. I have full confidence in you."

"It's more than for moral support. I always have fun when I'm with you. I'd like to go out together."

"Can you imagine the reaction if we showed up at your mom's campaign event together?" he said. "It would almost be worth breaking probation again. Ten bucks says at least one headline would mention the Capulets and Montagues."

"Nothing's worth you breaking probation again. But it would be pretty great."

"We wouldn't have to worry about your relationship with your mom because the sight of us together would probably be enough to kill her," Julian said.

"Nah. The rage fuel would strengthen her by supernatural amounts. She'd probably start growing multiple lives like a character in a video game."

He gave her a squeeze. "You need to go, baby. Quit stalling."

"I know." She pushed away from him and stood up. He clasped her hand and held her in place. "Hold up." He pulled out his phone and took a picture, looked at it, and shook his head. "Bronwyn, try to come up with some expression other than a prisoner on the way to the electric chair."

She laughed, and he snapped another photo. Apparently satisfied with that one, he walked her to the door. "Keep me informed."

"Are you sure you're going to be available?" she asked. "There's a *House Hunters* marathon on."

"It's *House Hunters International.* I hate that one, so it looks like I'm free." He kissed her forehead. "You've got this."

She nodded and forced a smile, stuffing down every negative thing she wanted to say.

On the way to the event, she blasted the radio. She hadn't driven her car in days. The last time she did so, she had been heading home to kill herself, and now everything was different. Drastically so, though in reality not much had changed. She was still jobless, still homeless. The difference, Bronwyn realized, was Julian. Having a friend, someone on her side who believed in her, had made all the difference in the world, and she knew without a doubt she was alive now because of him. Regardless of what happened tonight with Carlo and her mother, she had been affected enough to change her entire way of thinking. She wasn't a loser who couldn't do her job; she had merely been in the wrong job for the wrong reasons. She wasn't incapable or incompetent; she merely hadn't hit her stride yet. And thanks to Julian, she was no longer alone.

The drive to DC seemed unnaturally short, most likely because she didn't actually want to arrive. While still in the car, everything was theoretical. Once she set foot inside, it would be real. She would actually be attempting to assimilate herself into her mother's world; she would be trying to secure Carlo, a man she had dreamed of since she was a child.

She picked up the phone to text Julian she had made a huge mistake and was coming back home and saw he had already texted her. *You've got this.*

She took a deep breath and stuffed the phone in her purse. If Julian believed she could do it, maybe there was a chance she actually could. Before she could change her mind, she left the safety of her car and headed to the large building, pausing at security to be patted down and inspected. It seemed to take forever, so long she began to wonder if her mom had put her on some kind of list as a potential threat, as one of the crazy people who might one day show up and try to kill her. At last she was waved through. The guard opened the door for her.

"Here we go," she whispered to herself.

The banquet hall reminded her of her childhood, and she was immediately taken back to all the times she had gone to her mother's events. The dim lights and musty smell were the same, and they gave her the same feeling of institutional depression.

Julian had gone over everything with her until she got it. *Think of dating like a child's game of tag. If an adult were playing tag, we would locate the person we're trying to chase and make a direct beeline. Children don't play that way. They run around, back and forth, touching each other and darting away. You want to approach Carlo, make him aware of your presence, and dart away. Always leave him wanting more.*

"What about with my mother?" she had asked.

*Your mother is more of a man than I am, so play it the same. Show her what you've got, then disappear. By the time we're done with her, she'll want to crawl over broken glass to get you on her team. And don't let her get you alone because you're not ready for that; she'll break you.*

Bronwyn located her mother in the vast space. She eased her way over and stood beside her, inspecting the room. Eventually her mother turned to look at her and did a double take.

"Bronwyn?"

"Hi, Mom."

Her mother's eyes scanned her up and down, searching for the defect. For once she found none.

"What are you doing here?" Laurel asked.

"It's campaign season, Mom. The Porters are all in." She smiled at her mom and turned away while Laurel remained staring at her, her usually poised face a puzzled mask.

"Congresswoman, he's here," one of her aids hissed.

Bronwyn didn't have to ask who the "he" in question was. She saw Carlo the moment he entered the room.

"Why is he here?" Laurel asked.

"He was at the Baxter's event last night. Maybe he took our suggestion and is checking out both sides before he makes a commitment."

"Or maybe he's playing both sides," Laurel said, ever paranoid and suspicious.

Bronwyn alone knew why Carlo was there—because Julian had called and asked him to show up.

"We need an in. Give me an idea," Laurel said, snapping her fingers in the aid's face. While they debated the merits of who would make the first contact with Carlo, Bronwyn meandered across the room to him. He caught sight of her and watched her approach, his smile widening with every step.

"Carlo," she said.

"Hi."

"You stealing my lines?" she asked, and he laughed.

"There's no pillow here for me to borrow."

"Are you lost?" Bronwyn asked.

"Are you?"

"Do you always answer a question with a question?" she asked.

"Do you?" he replied.

She turned and caught sight of her mother's team, their whispered conference at a frenzy now. "I think my mother's getting the wrong idea about why you're here."

"I have no idea why I'm here, except Julian called and asked me to show up."

"Do you always do what Julian Baxter tells you to do?" she asked.

"Yes," he said. "Do you?"

"Lately. Well, it was exemplary to see you. Pro-tip: try the caviar, avoid the salmon." She turned to go. He caught her hand.

"That's it? You came all this way to say hello?"

"It was only a few steps. What else did you have in mind?" She was only partially turned toward him, but their hands were still clasped. His thumb smoothed gently over her fingers, dulling her brain. She fought hard against the sensation. Julian had been clear on keeping her wits about her.

"How about a dance?"

"I'm kind of busy. Lots of responsibilities for the Congress-woman's daughter, you know how it is."

"I'm starting to get the idea I might be here for you, and yet you're about to abandon me," he said.

She took a step closer and rested her palm on his chest. "Tell you what. If you're really good, I might save you a dance at the end of the evening."

"Define good," he said. His left hand skimmed her hip.

"You should say hello to my mother," she said, sidestepping the comment.

"I'll be sure and do that."

"Do me a favor?"

"What's that?"

She stood on her toes and whispered, her lips skimming his ear. "Tell her I sent you."

"What do I get if I do?" he asked.

"The satisfaction a good deed brings."

"For you, that will be enough. But only because I have a soft spot for old acquaintances."

"Acquaintances? Is that what we are, Carlo?"

"For now."

"Something to look forward to then." She patted his chest and walked away, certain his eyes were still on her.

# CHAPTER 12

**B**ronwyn sashayed away, pausing to talk to people she knew. She could feel the eyes of both Carlo and her mother on her, but she didn't turn to check. Instead she walked sedately out of the main hall, rounded, the corner, made sure the hallway was deserted, then sprinted to the bathroom and locked herself in a stall.

After doubling over to take a few deep breaths, she took out her phone and, with shaking fingers, texted Julian.

*Round one over, both points to me.*

He replied almost immediately.

*Excellent. Now leave the bathroom and get back out there.*

She laughed. *It's ridiculous how well you know me at this stage in our relationship,* she wrote.

*Think where we'll be in thirty years,* he replied. With a smile, she tucked the phone back into her purse and went back to the hall.

**A**s soon as she walked into the room, her mother caught her eye and motioned her over. Unable to think of a way out,

Bronwyn headed in that direction. But along the way, and to her surprise, people wanted to talk to her, friends of her mother that she hadn't spoken to in a long time, some not for years.

She realized, as she began to talk, how much she knew and remembered about each person, details she had no idea she knew until her brain provided them. A little while later, she had a new realization: she was working the room. She had watched her mother do it with precision for years. Bronwyn had never imagined herself doing the same thing, mostly because she had no desire to be in the spotlight. But for Bronwyn, it wasn't about making important political contacts. It was about connecting with people she had known for years, people who had long been part of her life but had fallen out of her immediate circle, due to time or proximity. It was nice to reconnect, almost nostalgic to catch up.

Eventually her mother grew impatient to talk to her and shot her *the look*, the one that said Bronwyn had better fall in line and comply or else. Bronwyn wasn't yet strong enough to stand up to *the look*. She finished the conversation she was having and headed toward her mother, but someone else stopped her along the way.

"Bronwyn, I haven't seen you in forever." It was one of her father's friends, a man who had seemingly been to every party and event her mother had ever hosted. He was a big part of Bronwyn's childhood, but unlike some she had always liked him.

"Judge Hill, how are you, sir?"

"Doing well."

"How is your mother? The last time we spoke, I believe she had started showing signs of dementia."

His face registered his surprise. "That must have been four years ago," he said. "I can't believe you remember."

"I remember meeting your mother once when I was little. She made an impression."

He smiled. "She has that effect. To answer your question, she hasn't been doing well at all, I'm afraid. Her memory is gone, and her body is failing. It's been…quite difficult, actually." His eyes were teary. She put her hand on his arm and gave it a sympathetic pat.

Laurel Portman watched as her daughter spoke to Jonah Hill, one of her husband's oldest friends and one of her biggest donors. Recently things had been a bit touchy between the two families, so she was especially tense when she saw Bronwyn stop and talk to him. When Jonah started to cry, she went into a near panic, wondering what on earth her most difficult child could have said to him to upset him so. Ditching the person she was speaking to without using her usual tact and polished manners, she hurried over to Bronwyn to try and salvage whatever she could from the meeting.

"Jonah, is everything okay?" Laurel asked. She rested her hand on Bronwyn's bicep as she approached, giving it a warning squeeze. She had no idea what her child was up to tonight, showing up unasked with a new style that suited her, but her track record led her to believe it was probably not good.

Jonah swiped at his eyes. "Bronwyn and I were discussing my mother. You may remember she hasn't been doing well." There was no mistaking the hint of accusation in the second part of his statement. Laurel bit the inside of her cheek, making a mental note to ream the nearest aid next time she saw him. How could she have forgotten to touch base over the sick mother? It was a sloppy mistake, and she was more than shocked Bronwyn had been the one to pick up the dropped ball. "Good girl you've got here, Laurel," he added, patting Bronwyn's shoulder as he stepped away from them.

"What are you up to?" Laurel snapped when Jonah was safely away.

"Just being myself, Mom."

Laurel would have said more, but Carlo approached. Evelyn Baxter had thrown down the gauntlet yet again by going after the boy. It was hitting below the belt to go after the maid's son in order to shore up the Latino vote or the Latinx vote, or whatever the politically correct term was nowadays, she could never remember, and now Laurel was left playing catch up trying to secure him to their side. She had been contemplating using Louisa's job as leverage when Bronwyn showed up with an apparent connection to the boy. *The man,* she reminded herself. Carlo had done well, earning a scholarship to a solid college, heading to law school and getting snapped up by a prestigious firm. In fact, the more she began to think about it, the more she began to picture him with Bronwyn. It could work to her advantage on a number of levels.

"It would seem to be the end of the evening, Bronwyn," Carlo said. "I think I've kept my end of the bargain."

"I can't say for certain, Carlo, because I haven't been watching you," Bronwyn said. "However, we Porters always keep our word and reward a job well done. Isn't that right, Congresswoman?"

"Yes," Laurel replied, but it came out sounding like a question. Somehow Bronwyn had taken charge of the conversation and, if appearances were correct, had Carlo eating out of the palm of her hand. She gave Carlo her hand. He led her onto the floor, and they started to dance. Even if Laurel had no vested interest in the situation, she would have thought they looked incredible together, like a power couple on the rise. After a rough adolescence, Bronwyn had come into her own. Tonight for the first time she seemed to have understood how to dress and do her hair to her most flattering advantage. Her look was on point—feminine, conservative without being stuffy. The flared dress highlighted her hourglass figure, drawing attention to her plus-sized bust without flaunting it grotesquely. It almost seemed as though Bronwyn had hired a stylist, but there was no way she could afford it, not on what she made.

Across the room the photographer who was in her pocket made eye contact with Laurel and raised his eyes in question. She gave him a nod, and he took a series of photos of Bronwyn and Carlo. Tomorrow they would be strategically placed in the society section of the paper. *Take that, Evelyn,* Laurel thought, and for the first time in either of their lives began to wonder if her fourth born could be someday be considered an asset and not a liability.

On the dance floor, Bronwyn settled into Carlo's clasp with the ease of someone who had been there many times before.

"I think this is the first time we've danced together," he noted.

"When would we have had opportunity before? When you thought of me as a pesky kid?" He was three years older, Julian's age.

"I never thought of you as pesky," he assured her.

"How did you think of me?"

"That might be a question for a later discussion," he said. "What are you doing after? Do you want to grab a coffee?"

"That sounds enticing, but I can't tonight. Sorry." Julian had told her that, no matter what, she was not to accept his first offer.

"Seeing you again makes me realize how much I've been missing out on. I think we need to get together and catch up."

"Are you suggesting we renew our friendship?"

"I'm suggesting we start with friendship and see where it takes us."

"I don't remember you being this flirtatious, Counselor."

"Maybe you've never given me the chance before," he said. "You've been gone a few years. I don't think I've seen you since…" he squinted, thinking, "you graduated college five years ago. Where have you been hiding, Bronwyn?"

"I've been in a secret location, prepping myself for this moment when we would meet again," she said.

"And the other morning was an unexpected test run?" he guessed.

"What other morning? I've blocked it from my mind," she said.

"I remember because you looked like you had just woken, and I thought, 'How cute Bronwyn is,' and I chastised myself for forgetting."

"If that's what you were thinking, then the meeting was a smashing success," she said.

"And what were you thinking as you looked at me with your oh-so-expressive eyes?" he asked.

"That might be a question for a later discussion," she said.

He pulled her slightly closer, erasing any space between them. "I'm free tomorrow. Are you free tomorrow?"

"We're always free, this is America," she noted.

"Are you trying to make me say the words?" he asked.

"Look at that, you know me better than you think," she said.

He smiled a little. "Bronwyn Porter, will you go out with me tomorrow, on a date?"

"Normally when a gentleman asks me for a date, I put him off a bit, make him squirm. But for an old acquaintance like you, I'll guarantee my availability," she said.

"And what of your mother?" he asked.

"If you'd like her to tag along I'll ask, but I can't say it won't be awkward."

"What will your mother think of you dating her maid's son?" he asked.

"Do you want the honest answer or the politically correct one?" she returned.

"Honesty, always."

"My mother's only concern, as always, is her career. She thinks you can help her get elected, and she would descend to the deepest pit of Hades and snag Satan himself for me to date, if she thought it would help her chances."

"Is that why you're here, to reel me in?"

"First, you're assuming I'd be able to reel you. You're a big fish, Carlo. Handsome, successful, good backstory. You can and should have any woman of your choosing. Second, you should know I would never go against my personal integrity to help my mother's campaign. Never, no matter what."

"Good to know she has one honest person on her team," he said. "As for your ability to reel me, for you, Bronwyn, I would be one of those fish who jumps into the boat of my own free will."

"I never imagined I would find having a discussion about fish so enticing," Bronwyn noted.

"Then by all means, let's talk more about fishing tomorrow," he said.

Though Bronwyn was reluctant to end the encounter, Julian had been clear she needed to be the first to walk away. "This dance has been…most informative, but I see my sister across the room, and I haven't spoken with her yet. So if you'll excuse me…" She stopped dancing and backed out of his embrace.

"I hoped to walk you to your car," he said.

Even without Julian to tell her no, Bronwyn wouldn't have wanted that to happen. Her car was a piece of junk. The dose of reality might remind them both her current façade was merely the illusion of a woman who had it all together.

"My mother is watching us. I'd prefer not to give her that much joy," she said. She kissed two fingers and touched them to his cheek before turning to walk away.

# CHAPTER 13

"Was that Carlo?" her oldest sister, Lena, stood at the edge of the room, too hugely pregnant to do more than shift uncomfortably from foot to foot.

"Yes," Bronwyn said.

"That kid grew up friggin' hot," Lena said.

"It's sweet to see how feminine and maternal this pregnancy has made you," Bronwyn said, and Lena laughed.

"All I'm saying is you'd better grab on to that boy and hang on for dear life."

Bronwyn tensed. "Did Mom tell you to say that?"

"You think mom wanted me to say Carlo is 'friggin' hot?'" Lena asked, incredulous.

"No, the other part about grabbing on."

"No, that was common sense. If grownup Carlo is anything like the boy he was, he's a good guy. And good guys who look like that aren't growing on trees."

"Can you imagine if they did? We'd plant so many of those trees we could repair the ozone in a day," Bronwyn said, and Lena laughed again, clutching her belly.

"I forgot how funny you are."

"Okay, I'm definitely sure mom didn't tell you to say that," Bronwyn said.

Lena surprised her by putting both arms around her shoulders and giving her a squeeze. "Don't let her get to you, little bit."

Bronwyn released a pent up breath and rested her head on Lena's shoulder. They'd never had a very sisterly relationship, so the moment was doubly nice and comforting.

"What are you up to these days?" Lena asked.

It was on the tip of Bronwyn's tongue to say something self-disparaging about what a loser she was, but she caught herself in time. "Getting myself together."

"Good for you," Lena said, giving her shoulders another squeeze. "Let's get together before the baby comes. I miss you."

"I miss you, too," Bronwyn said slowly, glancing over her shoulder to make sure her mother wasn't about to swoop in and intercept the moment.

Her phone buzzed with a text from Julian. She excused herself from Lena and pulled it out to read.

*Living vicariously means I'll die without input on what's happening.*

Smiling, she texted her reply. *A miracle happened.*

*Carlo proposed?* he guessed.

*No, my sister,* before she could finish the text, she was interrupted by someone else who wanted to have a word. By the time she retrieved her phone again, she was sitting in her car getting ready to drive home. She pulled out the phone and read his reply.

*Your sister proposed? You conservatives ARE knotty. PS. Plays on words work better in print.*

She was sleepy driving home, barely able to stay awake. But once there she parked the car, took off her shoes, and sprinted next door. Julian opened the door as if he'd been waiting for her and swept her into a hug that picked her feet up off the floor. She laughed as he twirled her around twice before setting her down.

"Was it everything you thought it would be?" he asked.

"And more," she agreed. She stood on her toes and kissed his cheek twice. "Thank you, straight godfather."

He grinned. "You're a rotten kid. And it's one in the morning, get out of my house. Have you no shame? Have you no home?"

"Yes, yes I do," she said, tossing her arms around him for one more tight hug before sprinting home.

When she let herself in her own house, she strolled through the living room and stopped short. Something was different, but what?

The pictures on the mantel had been rearranged. Bronwyn's picture was now front and center among them, and the photograph had been swapped out. Instead of her awkward sophomore class picture, it was the picture Julian took of her tonight—sophisticated, pretty, eyes sparkling with happiness. She picked the picture up, and hugged it to her, set it down again, and pulled out her phone to text Julian.

*PS. I adore you.*

*PS. You too, only more.*

*Not possible,* she replied.

*Bet me. Now go to bed, hobo. See also: profligate, drifter, vagrant, traveller.*

Laughing, Bronwyn took down her hair, shook it out, and continued on her way up the stairs to bed.

The next day was her date with Carlo. Bronwyn was nervous and trying not to be. "Any advice, coach?" she asked Julian.

"Yes. Hold on, I'll be back." He left the room and returned a minute later with something inside a paper bag. Bronwyn reached into the bag and pulled out a small cross-stitched sampler he'd made for her with a picture of a bumblebee and the words "BEE YOURSELF."

"I literally could not love it more," Bronwyn said. "Thank you."

"Have fun, but not too much, if you know what I mean. Carlo's a good Catholic boy. Don't scare him."

"Let's be honest, if he scares easy, he shouldn't be with me."

"Good point," he agreed.

By the time Carlo arrived, Bronwyn had talked herself down to reasonable levels of anxiety. And then she caught sight of him through the peephole of the front door.

"Bronwyn," he said, giving her a dazzling smile when she opened the door.

"Carlo. You look good enough to make me start stuttering hi again," she said. Leaning on the door looked like she was being casual, but in reality she needed the support. He really was an incredibly handsome man, the culmination of all her childhood dreams come true, minus the ones she'd had about Julian.

"You look, well, I might have to switch to my native tongue for a description," he said.

"Only you could say 'native tongue' and have it make you somehow even more appealing," she noted, and he laughed. She grabbed her purse and followed him to his car.

"Would it be a cliché if I took you to a Mexican restaurant?" he asked.

"Would it be a cliché if I ordered a huge meal then ate none of it because I devoured my weight in chips and salsa?" she asked.

"Yes, but I'd be disappointed if you didn't."

The car ride was comfortable as they got caught up on old acquaintances, mostly her family. "How do you know Julian?" he asked.

"We've become friends," she said.

"Are you having a post-adolescent rebellious stage?" he asked.

"If being friends with Julian is rebellion, I don't want to be right," she said.

"Me neither," he agreed.

They were seated quickly at the restaurant and made their selection. "So," Bronwyn began after their waitress left. "Tell me what life is like for my friend, Carlo."

"I can't complain. I have an active social life."

"Is that code for 'the ladies love Carlo?'" she interjected.

"I do all right. But there's no one special. Yet."

"And your job," she prompted. "Do you enjoy being a lawyer?"

"I love it. If all goes well, I hope to make partner by my thirty fifth birthday."

She whistled softly. "Look at you with a five year plan. Impressive. Between that, your heart-stopping good looks, and the accent, you're literal man candy."

"I don't think that's what man candy means," he said.

"It is in my book, and I've always had a sweet tooth." She gave him an exaggerated wink and brushed his knuckles with her fingers.

"Wow, Bronwyn, you are bringing the heat," he said.

"Everyone has a specialty in life. Mine is crippling men with my devastating flirting skills," she said, reaching for a chip as soon as the waitress set them down.

"I believe it," he said. "What about you? No five year plan?"

"I've been told not to talk about my five year plan on a date because men find it terrifying," she said.

"Short of learning you perform human sacrifices, I can't imagine what would be terrifying. What's your plan?"

She tilted her head at him, considering. "In five years, I'd like to have at least one child, hopefully more. And, for the record, I'm only telling you that because we go back a ways and not because I have your wedding tux picked out."

"No career plans?" he asked.

She sighed. "What can I tell you, Carlo? What I lack in ambition, I make up for in awkwardness." She glanced quickly around, almost expecting Julian to appear and bite her.

Carlo, however, didn't seem put off by her self-deprecating statement. "No plans to follow your mother into politics?"

"I would rather drop an anvil on my foot than ever follow my mother into politics," she said, leaning forward over the table as a signal of her intensity.

"For the record, I agree with you."

"You would rather drop an anvil on my foot than follow my mother into politics?" she guessed.

"I would like to have at least one child by the time I make partner, hopefully more," he said. "Many of the women I've dated consider children a liability. But I'm from a large, Catholic family. Children are a gift, a blessing."

Outwardly she gave him a sedate smile. Inside, her ovaries were pulsating as if they knew they were being called to active duty. "Hmm." She loaded a chip with salsa and stuffed it in her mouth to avoid leaping over the table and tackling him.

As she had guessed, she ate so many chips and salsa she had no room for her meal. "I'll box it up and take it to Julian," she said.

"Switch the salsas. Julian doesn't like tomatillos."

"You guys are close," she observed.

"Close enough to know each other's salsa preferences, you mean?"

She nodded.

"We were unlikely friends as kids, but we found we had a lot in common. The drug and alcohol years were hard. I'm glad he's past them."

"I didn't know him then."

"You wouldn't have liked him," Carlo said. "No one did."

"What was he like?"

"Impulsive, thoughtless, self-centered, careless, depressed, angry, reckless."

"Basically the opposite of everything he is now."

"Yes," he agreed.

"Why did you stay friends with him?" she asked.

"What is the point of friendship if not loyalty?" he asked.

"Oh, geez," she said, fanning herself with her napkin.

"What?" he asked, grinning in anticipation of her answer.

"You're as pretty on the inside as you are on the outside, aren't you?" she said.

"Answering in the affirmative would kill any humility I've tried to posses, but yes."

"You've got to give me something, some negative fault to hold onto," she said.

"If I tell you, you must swear never to repeat it," he said.

She made a zipping motion over her lips.

He leaned forward and lowered his voice. "I weep like a small child at those ASPCA commercials."

She blinked at him. "That's it? That's what you believe is your worst flaw? That you're sensitive and can't stand to see animals suffer? You're killing me." She started to scoot out of the booth, but he held her back.

"Your turn."

"My turn for what?"

"Your turn to tell me something negative, to give me something to hold onto."

She opened her mouth to ask him why he would need something like that when her deficiencies were so glaring, but it was as if Julian's disapproving spirit transported to sit beside her and shake his head, forcing the words back before she could speak them. Was it possible Carlo was as attracted to her as she was to him? "Are you ready? It's very bad."

He nodded.

She leaned forward and took his hand. "I tend to fall too hard for guys who cry at sad puppy commercials."

His smile was slow, reaching his eyes and lighting his face. He brought her hand to his mouth and kissed it. "Well, then, let's go find a TV."

She returned his smile, skimming his cheek with her palm. When they left the restaurant, he took her hand, clasping it in an ambiguous way that might have been either friendly or possessive. A noise behind them made them pause and turn. A man with a camera lowered it and darted into an alley.

"I don't believe it," Bronwyn muttered.

"Friend of yours?" Carlo asked.

"My mother's handiwork." She pinched her eyes closed. "I don't believe this." The pictures of her and Carlo dancing had made the paper this morning, but Bronwyn had hoped that would be the extent of her mother's involvement, at least for now. She should have known better. Her mother had never been able to leave well enough alone when it came to her.

"Would you like me to go, shall we say, confiscate his camera?" Carlo asked.

Bronwyn's eyes popped open. "You would do that?"

"If you'd like," he said.

"I think the mental image of that will be enough to propel me through many hard times in my life, but, no. I don't want you to do that."

"What would you like me to do?" he asked.

She rested her palm on his chest. "As I see it we have two options: We could end the date and go home."

"I already prefer the second option," he said.

"All right, then let's give him something worthwhile to take pictures of," she said. She reached up and smoothed her finger over his lips.

"What did you have in mind?" he asked. Was it her hopeful imagination or did he sound a bit unsteady?

"Watch and see," she said, taking his hand and tugging him to the car.

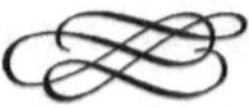

# CHAPTER 14

"I have to say, Bronwyn, this is definitely not what I thought you had in mind."

"And I have to say, Carlo, you make that hairnet look sexy," Bronwyn returned. After they learned the reporter was following them, they drove to the local homeless shelter and volunteered to serve the evening meal and clean up. Now, three hours later, their work was done. She sniffed her arm. "I smell like French fries."

"It works for you," Carlo said, leaning close to inhale. "Should we see if our friend is still hovering outside?"

She nodded and allowed him to lead her outside. The reporter was gone. "I admit I'm a bit disappointed. I hoped to see what else you might find for us to do."

"I think I'm ready to be away from an audience for a while," she said.

They grabbed a cup of coffee and walked along the river. Conversation remained light and easy and pleasant. He drove her home and walked her to the door.

"It feels odd to approach the front door," he said, his eyes roaming around the porch as if he'd never seen it before.

Bronwyn had never thought much of the fact that he always used the back door. It was the door Louisa used, but it was also the door the family used. She had always considered it the family entrance, but she wondered if Carlo saw it differently, as the servant's entrance. She put her hand on his arm.

"Carlo, I hope we never made you feel anything less than a part of us, than family."

"*You* never did, Bronwyn," he said. He took a step closer. A ball of tension ignited and simmered between them. Bronwyn wanted to toss herself at him, but Julian had been clear about holding on to the tension and letting it build.

"I have to warn you I'm a good conservative girl. That means no kissing on the first date." It was a bit of a lie—she had kissed on the first date lots of times. But a lot of those dates ended up being one-time events, and so she was trying to do everything different now. Before, her biggest problem was she always fell too hard, too fast, mostly because she had been desperate for love and relationship. But the new friendship with Julian had filled a lot of those holes in her life, and she no longer felt the mad desire to fling herself at the nearest eligible man. For the first time she felt thoughtful, ready to take it slow and make sure Carlo was all he appeared to be and they were well suited. She was holding herself in check, both mentally and emotionally, refusing to picture their future children or practice writing *Bronwyn Garcia* in her head. This time she would only assume they were friends, until one or both of them deemed otherwise.

"Something to look forward to for next time then," Carlo said. He stepped forward and kissed her cheek and lingered for a second, his breath blowing warm on her cheek. Even pheromones were on his side because the smell of him was enough to make her want to toss her earlier statement aside, press him against the wall, and kiss him until someone declared a winner. In order to not do that, she remained silent and still until he took a step back and then jogged lightly down the steps to his car.

She remained on the porch, giving him a little wave as he backed out of the drive. Once he was gone, she glanced at the Baxter house, debating a visit with Julian. Holding so much in check had left her exhausted. All she wanted now was her bed.

Wearily, she made her way into the house. A sound from the entertainment room brought her up short. Someone was talking. Had one of her family members come home? Wary now, she eased into the room and saw Julian sitting on the couch playing video games.

"Hey, how was the date?" he asked.

"What if I'd invited him in with me?" she asked.

"Then we would have had to crack open the Porter gun cabinet and duel with pistols over you."

She sank onto the couch beside him. "It was good."

He paused the game and inspected her. "Not good?"

"No, good. I'm tired. It took a lot of energy to be myself but not too much."

He smiled and faced the TV. "Sounds like you struck the perfect balance. What did you guys do?"

"We went out to eat. I brought you food."

"Ooh, gimme. I'm starving."

She retrieved the leftovers for him and sank back into the couch while he started to eat.

"What did you do after the restaurant? You were gone forever."

"We worked at a soup kitchen."

He froze, fork halfway to his mouth. "You worked at a soup kitchen on a first date?"

She shrugged. "My mom tipped off a reporter who followed us. Instead of trying to shake him, we gave him something worthwhile to photograph."

"Was that your idea?" he asked.

She nodded. "Was it bad?"

"No, it was brilliant. When your mom calls you tomorrow, tell her you'll only work for her if she pays you."

She snorted a laugh.

"I'm serious."

"None of us have ever gotten paid for working on the campaign," she said.

"Then it's about time you did. Plus it will garner her respect."

"And her annoyance."

"Then it's a double win," he said. He took another bite and chewed and swallowed in silence. "How was the kiss?"

"Didn't kiss him."

He gave her the surprised look again. "He didn't try?"

"He would have, but I told him I didn't kiss on the first date."

"Wow," he breathed.

"Was that bad, too?"

"No, that was also good. Carlo is old fashioned, and he likes girls who are, too. Plus you're giving him a challenge. But I'm both shocked and impressed by your discipline. I mean, he's been your dream guy for a long time. You finally had an opportunity, and you held out."

"It was easier than I thought it would be. Do you think that's bad?"

He chuckled. "No, baby, I do not think that's bad."

She reached for the fork and took a bite of the food she'd been too stuffed to eat earlier. "I'm pretty sure I locked up before I left."

"I broke in. It was fun, like old times."

"You used to break into places?"

"Yes. A lot."

"Why?"

"Sometimes for fun. Sometimes to steal things to sell for drugs."

"I thought you have a trust fund."

"When the drug years were at their worst, my tricky lawyer put restrictions on my trust. I had to go to him any time I wanted money. Guy was suspicious and tightfisted. So I stole stuff. And now that I'm clean, my money is still intact. Once again, I come out disproportionately on top."

"You're sitting in my parents' living room at midnight playing video games alone while wearing an ankle monitor. I wouldn't say you got off scot free," she said.

"I thought your mom campaigned against violent video games," he said.

"She did."

"And yet I'm playing one of the most violent ones on the market in her living room."

"Really? In her defense, she probably has no idea where it came from. Come to think of it, neither do I."

"Probably one of your brothers sneaked it in," he said.

"Nah, my brothers are all choirboys."

He snorted a laugh. "No, they're not."

"How do you know?" she asked.

"I know," he said.

"What do you know?"

"Honey, we're neighbors. We run in the same circles. I know a lot about your family. Too much, actually."

"You probably know more about my family than I do," she said.

"Truth." He finished the food, set it aside, and put his arm around her. She put both arms around him and rested her head on his shoulder. His fingers gently toyed with the hair at her neck. "Do you want to keep going with this?"

"Yes, it's relaxing," she murmured.

"I didn't mean *this*. I meant do you want to keep going with the plan?"

She sat up to look at him slightly. "Why wouldn't I?"

"It's going to hurt," he said.

She frowned, confused. "I thought the point is to make it feel better."

"It's going to get worse before it gets better," he said.

"I don't understand."

"You said there are things I know about your family you don't. When you find out, it's going to hurt. It's going to change the way you see the world. I guess I need to know you're doing this willingly, that I'm not dragging you into it."

Her heart began to thunder with an unnamed dread. "I want to finish what we've started. I feel like I'm on a journey now, and I need to see it through."

"Okay." They sat in silence a while longer, his fingers gliding gently along her neck. "Bronwyn."

"Mmm." She was so relaxed, she was nearly asleep.

"Do you really not kiss on the first date?"

"I kiss on the first date. I kiss at first sight. I once kissed a stranger on an elevator because I thought he was winking at me. Turned out he had pinkeye and I got it, too."

He laughed. "Geez."

"Do you kiss on the first date?" she asked.

"It's been so long since I had a first date I don't remember," he said.

"Soon the monitor will come off and you can start going out again," she said. She felt a bit melancholy about that. Right now he was all hers, and she selfishly liked it that way.

"There's no one here. I'll probably have to go back to my apartment in the city."

"You have an apartment in the city? Why are you here and not there?"

"Because this has always felt more like home," he said.

"Yes," she agreed. Her parents had a house in DC as well, but the peaceful country house on the river had always felt more like real life. "Julian?"

"Yes."

"Can we stop talking about when you go away?" she asked.

"How about we stop talking altogether and watch mindless, brain-rotting television?"

"Yes, please."

He picked up the remote and pushed a button. When he set it back down, he pulled the afghan over them and slipped his arm back around her. Bronwyn yawned. Julian followed suit, and a few minutes later they were asleep.

# CHAPTER 15

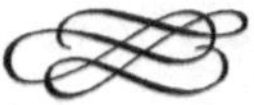

True to Julian's prediction, Laurel Porter called the next morning.

"When were you going to tell me you got fired?" was her opening question.

"Probably never," Bronwyn said. There was no need—her mother was so deeply involved in her life, the news would get back to her eventually, and it had.

"And you lost your apartment," Laurel continued.

"Yes," Bronwyn agreed.

"And you're staying at the summer house. Without permission."

*Looks like we're all caught up, Mom. Good talk.* Bronwyn bit back the sarcastic reply, knowing it wouldn't do anything but anger her mother. So far she sounded normal. The statements about her life's failures were more of a way of taking stock of Bronwyn's most recent screw-ups. "Mom, may I please stay at the summer house a while?" Bronwyn asked.

Laurel sighed. "I suppose, as long as we're both clear it's temporary. You need to stand on your own two feet."

*As soon as you decide what those feet are and where they should go, you mean?* Bronwyn thought and was surprised by the bitterness of her inner monologue. For as long as she could remember her parents had pushed independence and personal responsibility. But for all of that time her mother had also been swooping in, trying to control and arrange everything for her. How could she possibly hope to be independent when her mother refused to allow her to do anything on her own? Julian was right; she and her mother both shared the blame for her failures.

"As long as you're between jobs, I think you should come work on the campaign," Laurel said.

*Here we go.* "That sounds great, Mom."

There was a pause. "It does?"

"Yes. Let's talk salary."

Another pause, longer this time. "You're my daughter."

"Yes, your daughter who needs a job and is a good, hard worker. If I'm working for you, I won't be available to look for other employment, and a girl's gotta live on something."

Laurel sighed. "I will talk to Jeffrey about it." Jeffrey Clark was her campaign manager. "We'll have to clear any legal loopholes."

"Sounds good."

When the next pause came, Bronwyn smiled because she could sense her mother gearing up to be solicitous. "How long have you and Carlo been a thing?"

"We've been friends since childhood," Bronwyn said, taking pleasure in the reminder. Her mother had never outright said she didn't want Bronwyn befriending the maid's son, but it had been the unspoken impression. In any case, Bronwyn had never touted her friendship with Carlo to her mother in case she forbade it.

"It seems you're more than friends now," Laurel said.

"The potential is there, perhaps, but for now it's only friendship."

"Hmm. I don't have to tell you, or maybe I do, this is a difficult campaign. Evelyn and I are neck and neck. One tiny thing could tip the scales in either direction."

"That sounds exhausting," Bronwyn said.

Laurel paused again. "It is, yes. The point is Carlo could be quite helpful to either side. I feel he should be ours because of our family connection. I'd like you to do whatever you can to make that happen."

"Mom, Carlo is a grown man and he'll make his own decisions about which way to vote," Bronwyn said.

"Come now, Bronwyn, there are always things we can do to change a man's thinking," her mom said. Bronwyn grimaced at the phone. Was this her mother or her pimp?

"Gross, Mom."

Laurel huffed. "I didn't mean that. I meant you have wiles. Use them."

"I thought you wanted me to save my wiles for marriage."

Laurel actually laughed at that. "All I'm saying is he seems charmed by you. Use it."

"I have to be honest with you, Mom. I have no plans to try and manipulate Carlo into anything for the sake of your campaign. Whatever is going on with him in my private life will be separate from my work on your behalf. If that's not acceptable to you, then you'd better not hire me because I won't change my mind."

"Don't get huffy," Laurel said. "Keep Carlo to yourself, but a good word on my behalf now and then wouldn't hurt."

"Fine. I'll be sure and highlight some of your better policies for him next time we get together," Bronwyn said, and Laurel seemed satisfied.

"I was also thinking since you'll be working in DC, you might as well stay here in town with me and Dad."

"No," Bronwyn blurted. "I mean no. I mean thank you, but no." She shuddered, fighting her gag reflex. Her soul could not survive staying with her parents in DC, and she wasn't ready to leave Julian, not by a long shot.

"It's going to be a long drive to and from the city, Bronwyn," her mother snapped, as if Bronwyn had no idea how long it took to commute.

"More time to sing in the car. I'm getting really good, thinking of becoming a professional car singer when the campaign is over," Bronwyn said.

Her mother, of course, didn't laugh. Her family had always viewed Bronwyn's sense of humor as yet another liability.

"Fine. I'll see you tomorrow," her mother said and disconnected. Bronwyn remained frozen, staring at nothing.

Julian let himself in. "Were we playing freeze tag, and I forgot?"

"My mother called. I start work tomorrow."

"Oh. You sound dismal. This is what you wanted, isn't it?"

"Yes," she said, but it came out sounding like a question. "She asked me to move back to DC."

"Are you going to?"

"Not by the hair of my chinny chin chin," she said.

"Huh." He tipped her face to his and leaned close, inspecting.

Bronwyn's heart started to thump hard. "What are you doing?"

"Making sure there's no actual hair on your chin. That's no way to start a new job where you're supposed to be impressive. We're good, you're smooth." He kissed her chin, just below and to the left of her lips. Bronwyn swallowed reflexively and grasped his lapels to keep from tipping over. "Okay?" he asked, righting her with a hand to her bicep.

"Yes."

"You know what I think is going on here?" he said.

"What?" she whispered.

"I think maybe you have an inner ear imbalance. You should get that looked at." He let her go and opened the fridge, reaching for a bottle of water. "Ugh, plastic. I'm buying all the Porters reusable water bottles for Christmas." He opened the water and took a chug.

"Hypocrite alert," Bronwyn said, pointing to the plastic bottle in his clasp.

"It's okay. After my probation is over, I'm planning to take the family jet to a climate conference in Bali," he said.

"Ah, you've clearly got a handle on the hypocrisy."

"You should come with me. Bali's nice. Of course by then you and Carlo could be engaged, and he probably wouldn't like the idea of you traipsing across continents with your male friend. Hmm." He took another swig of water and eyed her. The bubble of tension was there, only now it was at sauté instead of simmer.

"You know, Julian," she said softly, taking a step toward him. "Maybe we've got it all wrong."

"How so?" The water in his hand was temporarily forgotten as he stared at her.

"Maybe you," she touched her finger to his navel, "need to give me," she added her other finger beside it, "the family jet so Carlo and I can honeymoon together in Bali."

He blinked at her as if his mind was being pulled from a fog. Then he smiled and gave her shoulder a light push. "You're a bad kid. Now make me a sammich."

"Excuse me, what?"

"Isn't that what you conservative girls live for? Some strong man to order you around and give your life purpose?"

"I'm clearly the first conservative girl you've ever known," she said. "But as luck would have it, I'm also starving, so sit down." She made lunch, and then they went for a swim. After that they ordered in for supper and ate in melancholy silence.

"It feels like the end of something," Bronwyn said.

"I'm going to miss your incessant and inane chatter," he said.

"Aw, you're so sweet," she said.

"Plus your face and basically everything else about you," he added.

"This way we'll have something to talk about in the evenings," she said.

"You'll get home late," he reminded her.

She shook her head. "I'm planning to work the minimal amount and cut out early every day."

"Tell me more about being a productive member of society," he said.

"Ain't nepotism grand?" she said, sprawling onto the couch with her feet up. He stretched out beside her, his feet twining with hers on the coffee table.

"Regardless of my selfish desire to keep you all to myself, you're going to kill it. You've got this, Bronwyn."

"I feel like for the first time, maybe I do," she said. "It's like the blinders are coming off, and I'm starting to understand things in my life better, things I've been too close to to get a clear picture before. I know that's because of you, Julian, and I really appreciate it."

"Don't thank me until all this is over and the dust has settled. You may wish to go back," he said.

"No, I don't ever want to go back. Ignorance is not bliss, it's just ignorance. And, regardless of the outcome, I have you now. That's worth more to me than anything else I might get out of the bargain."

"Are you saying that because we're both lonely and desperate and all we have is each other?" he asked.

"What other reason could there be?" she asked.

"Exactly," he agreed. "When I get free of this monitor, I'm going to ditch you so hard, it will be like we never met."

"I would expect nothing less. And when I'm fabulous and married to Carlo, I'll forget you ever existed."

"For your sake, I demand it," he said, picking her up and settling her in his lap. "Until then, we have all these hours to fill and nothing to do. Suggestions?"

"I think you know what I want," she said, her finger skimming a trail over his ear.

"Again?" he asked.

She nodded, biting her lip.

"You're insatiable," he said. He reached for the remote, turned on *House Hunters,* and they settled in for a long night of watching.

CHAPTER 16

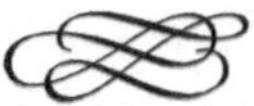

**B**ronwyn's day was off to a spectacular start. She woke to a bouquet of flowers by her bed and a note from Julian.

*You've got this. PS. Adore you more. PPS. Might be time to invest in a better security system, seeing as how you're such a heavy sleeper. PPPS. You sleep cute. PPPPS. I'll miss you. PPPPPS. How many of these before it becomes annoying?*

She smiled and caught sight of the razor blade, still on her nightstand. It was out of place next to the beautiful arrangement of flowers; it was out of place in her life. Carefully, she dropped it into her trash, bundled up the bag, and carried it to the outside can to save herself the temptation of digging it back out again.

She made it to her mother's campaign headquarters early. It felt different to arrive as an employee and not a child visiting her parent. After supplying the personnel manager with her information, she began assimilating into her new position. It was strange to see her mother through fresh eyes. Bronwyn had spent so much of her life viewing her as a terrifying bully. It was interesting to watch her in action as an employer. She was formidable, clear of mind, and strong of opinion. People flitted around her like she was the first female pope, ready and willing to do her bidding. That fact was made more impressive by the knowledge that only a few of them were paid employees; the rest were volunteers.

Her mother's specialty was cutting to the chase and inspiring people. She had a way of speaking truth that made people sit up and take notice. During her time in congress, she had been a fearless bulldog and, even as a freshman, had put the fear into men twice her age with twice the experience. It had likely been a hard blow when, after being re-elected multiple times, Evelyn Baxter won her seat back. Some might feel defeated. Bronwyn's mother took it as a challenge. She was out for blood this time around.

"Bronwyn, good you're here." Her mother's campaign manager, Jeffrey Clark, greeted her with a hug. "I've been telling Laurel for years she ought to bring you on." It was a lie, Bronwyn knew, because practically everything Jeffrey said was a lie. He was the consummate campaign manager, always ready to tickle the ears of whoever was listening. If the tides turned against her, Bronwyn knew Jeffrey would be the first to tell Laurel to cut her loose. Though, as she looked around the room, she wondered if there was a bit of truth in his words. No one else from the family was there, save for her mother. It was stark contrast to earlier campaigns when everyone had been involved fielding phone calls, stuffing envelopes, and doing anything else that needed done. All six children along with their father had been Laurel's biggest supporters. Now she had a staff, including Bronwyn.

"Hi, Jeffrey. How are you?"

"I never change. It's what makes me a good political aid," he said.

"And how is Patricia?" she asked, trying to remember the last time she saw Jeffrey's wife. She couldn't, but then Patricia was that kind of woman—easily forgettable.

"Perfectly fine, dear. Are you ready to get started today?"

"Absolutely," Bronwyn said. "What did you have in mind for me?"

"I don't have to tell you the millennial and Gen Z votes are critical and hard won. That's your generation." The statement sounded like an accusation, as if Bronwyn were personally responsible for keeping the young vote away. "It is without a doubt our weakest link. The pro-life numbers are growing while our numbers keep dropping. It's maddening." He led her over to a group of people about her age, give or take a few years. "We've been strategizing some social media events, some concerts, things of that nature. That's where you come in. This is your team now, you're in charge. Carry on, and good luck."

Just like that, he dropped her off and walked away, leaving six people staring at her with a mix of wariness and resentment. "Who knows what nepotism is?" she asked, and all of them raised their hands. "Good, we can skip the elephant in the room and get down to business. My name is Bronwyn. I'd love to hear your names and what you've been working on."

They told her, and she made notes on that, as well as her observations. Her team all came equipped with stainless steel water bottles. Everyone her mother's generation or older carried a disposable plastic water bottle.

When it was near the end of the day, she asked for a meeting with her mother and Jeffrey, both of whom seemed more curious than interested in what she had to say.

"The team has some interesting social media events coming up," she began, having learned early it was always better to start with a positive.

"Good," Jeffrey said. "Excellent."

"There's a slight problem, however. Actually more than one. Mom, you don't do your own social media."

"No one does," she said.

"Not true. Lots of people do. The most successful ones are done by real people."

"No one can tell the difference," Laurel replied.

"Again, not true. Everyone of my generation and younger can tell the difference."

"I'm busy, Bronwyn. I don't have time for that kind of thing."

Bronwyn held up her hands in surrender. "That may be, but I'm telling you if you want to connect with a younger demographic, you need to start doing at least a few yourself. Post a few family pictures on Instagram. Tweet something positive or funny that happens throughout your day. Send a shoutout to MoonPie."

"What's MoonPie?" Laurel asked as Jeffrey added, "What's a shoutout?"

"MoonPie, you know, the cookie? Their social media is hot right now. It's trendy and fun to be on the bandwagon."

"You want me to talk to a cookie?" Laurel said.

"It's part of being more approachable, more real and authentic. Authenticity is what I want to talk to you about. We need to get rid of all the plastic in the office."

"Why?" Jeffrey and Laurel said together.

"For the planet," Bronwyn said.

Laurel rolled her eyes. "I think Evelyn has that track covered."

"No, it's not about party lines anymore. Everyone in my generation grew up hearing about recycling, Earth Day, saving the planet, reusing our resources, melting ice caps, dying polar bears, and climate change. It's not a party line thing; it's a generational thing. You need to show young voters you're committed to it and understand. Also, start carrying your own reusable water bottle everywhere you go. Ask for it instead of disposable plastic bottles in all but the most extreme circumstances. I guarantee that will get a notice," Bronwyn promised.

Her mother still looked annoyed, but Jeffrey sat forward, intrigued. "Go back to authenticity. I hear that word a lot bandied about by my kids, and I never applied it to the campaign before. Laurel, I think she may be on to something."

"Why hasn't anyone else on the team said it to us before now?" Laurel asked.

"Because you terrify them," Bronwyn replied. "Mom, you need to soften up a little. I'm not saying you should take a softer stance on policy, but you don't want to be Leona Helmsley. You have four, soon to be five, grandchildren. Bring them into the spotlight a bit. Take them to the playground, and put a selfie on social media. Your platform is family values, so highlight your family. And while we're on the topic, authenticity needs to be in every area of your platform. My generation can sniff out hypocrisy ten miles away. If you say you support family values, then do so."

"What did you have in mind, Bronwyn?" The question came from Jeffrey. He seemed far more interested in Bronwyn's speech than her mother was, but she and Jeffrey had zero baggage with each other.

"The biggest criticism coming from the left is our support of life ends at birth. It's not enough to be pro-life anymore. We need to be pro-adoption, pro getting kids out of foster care and into families, pro supportive of single mothers and fathers, pro disability, pro special Olympics, and pro people in nursing homes. If we really believe each life has value, we need to be committed to showing it, pre-birth to natural death."

"I'd elect you," Jeffrey declared, smacking his palm on the table. "By gum, Laurel, we might have a successor in the making. Where've you been hiding Bronwyn all these years?"

"It's a mystery," Laurel said, her tone dry.

Bronwyn had more thoughts and ideas, but she thought she'd said enough to begin with. It amazed her a bit how much she had picked up from watching her mother through the years, things she didn't even know she knew. And lately she'd been thinking about things Julian had said, mostly about hypocrisy. She had never put a name to it, but she felt the same way about people who presumed to be anything less than what they said they were. Until Julian put it into words, she thought it was a personal quirk.

Near the end of the day, she felt a tap on her shoulder. When she turned, Carlo stood behind her.

"Oh, my goodness, what are you doing here?" she said, tossing her arms around him in an impromptu hug of surprise.

"A little birdie told me you were working here now," he said.

"My mom?" she said, cringing at the prospect of her mother's continued interference.

"My mom," he said. "For some reason she thought I'd be keenly interested to know you're working a mere five blocks from my firm now. Turns out she was right."

"Only five blocks? That's perfect stalking distance," she said, and he laughed.

"For you or for me?" he said.

"Let's trade off," she suggested.

"Since today seems to be my turn, would you like to grab dinner?"

"I'd love to. Let me text our mutual friend and let him know I'll be late."

He waited while she finished up, and they walked to a nearby restaurant together.

"How was your day, Bronwyn? I was surprised when my mother told me you were working for your mother. It seemed an odd choice, given you said you'd rather, what was it, drop an anvil on your foot than go into politics."

"I still don't want to go into politics, but they are my mother's life. I long ago accepted the fact she loves them more than she loves me. If I ever want to have a relationship with her or even attempt to under-stand her, I need to embrace what she does. This is me, embracing."

"How was it?"

She leaned in and looked both ways before answering. "It was a blast."

"Really?" he said, leaning in, mimicking her position. Absently, his fingers slid over hers in a sweet, intimate little caress that left her staring at their combined fingers instead of answering the question. He tapped her index finger, and she returned her attention to his smiling face.

"I'm heading up a team. You don't know my work history, so let me tell you that has never happened to me before, and they're all so nice and fun and every good thing, like the type of people I would be friends with even if I didn't have to like them for work. And, I don't know, things make sense. It's like I've stepped inside the Matrix, and I can understand everything as it's supposed to be. I'm seeing it in real time, the things my mom's campaign needs to work on. Like I've been bitten by a radioactive spider that has imbued me with special polit-ical powers."

"Wow," he said.

"Sorry, that was a lot of blurting on my part," she said. "How was your day?"

"Ordinary, compared to yours. Lots of lawyer stuff, boring."

"I've read enough John Grisham to know that's not true. Did you defeat a corrupt corporation today? Solve the murder of a sitting Supreme Court judge? Which one?"

"I researched and wrote a brief."

"*The Pelican Brief?*"

"Do you want me to make something up so my mundane job seems exciting?" he asked.

"Could you?"

"Today I discovered the giant firm I work for has ties to the Russian mafia and spent my lunch hour running for my life and arranging a new identity."

"I knew it," she said. "I'll miss you."

"Why do you assume I didn't get one for you, too? I go, you go, *chica.*"

"Yes, throw some Spanish in there. That's what this conversation needed to make you sexier. Seriously, you could read the warning labels on a paint can and it would be drool worthy," she said.

"Bronwyn, you're a loon," he said, chuckling.

"Who told? Have you been in contact with my exes? Was it George? Because I swear I didn't know that gun was loaded," she said.

"I can definitely see why you and Julian have become friends. You two together must be a laugh riot," he said.

"We do all right."

Their food arrived. Conversation remained light and fun, as if they'd resumed their childhood friendship with no interruption. They hadn't been close, but they'd been the kind of pals who had a few laughs and occasionally shared a few real conversations. It was easy to think that was all they were now.

But then the dinner ended and Carlo walked her back to her car. "This is your car?" he asked, tapping her decade-old sedan.

"This is my car," she admitted, trying not to be embarrassed. He had a new car that was both expensive and tasteful. "It kind of looks like your car's dilapidated grandpa, doesn't it?"

"No, it looks like the car of a person who works hard for a living. I've always admired that your parents didn't simply give you things, that you had to earn them."

"I've never minded," *until now,* she mentally added. She had never been so down on her luck before. It would have been nice to have a softer place to fall. At least she had the summer house as a point of reference until she found something else, whenever that might be. The job with her mother only paid a pittance, certainly not enough to get her own place in the city.

"I feel like I've lost you," Carlo said.

Bronwyn drew her attention back to him. "I'm sorry. My mind wandered to poverty for a moment."

"Is it back now?" he asked.

"Yes, I am fully here and in the moment," she promised.

"Good," he said, and then he kissed her. It was a good kiss, amazing, really. Bronwyn wasn't the only one who thought so because when it finished, he pressed her against the car and kissed her again, and then a third time, lightly.

"Did I mention my mother's tough on crime?" she whispered, more than a little breathless.

"What?" he asked. Was he also a bit breathless, or was that her imagination?

"I promised her I would talk up some of her good points."

"Was that it?" he asked.

"Yes." She stood on her toes, plunged her fingers into his hair, and kissed him until he broke it off, definitively breathless.

"I'll call," he promised. He kissed her forehead and stepped away. With other guys, Bronwyn would be dubious about the claim, but she knew Carlo was a man of his word. If he promised to call, he would call.

"I'll answer," she said and then blew him a kiss and got into her car.

# CHAPTER 17

Over the next few weeks, Bronwyn's life settled into a predictable pattern. She worked for her mother's campaign. Her downtime was split between Julian and Carlo, with whom she was making slow and steady progress as a couple.

One day when she arrived home, completely exhausted, she let herself into Julian's house and plopped on his couch.

"Hard day at the salt mines?" he asked, setting aside his needlework.

"The canary died. Spoiler alert: in this metaphor, I am the canary," she said, closing her eyes and resting her head on the back of the couch.

"What do you want to do for supper?" he asked. When she wasn't with Carlo, it was assumed they would eat together.

"I can cook somethin'," she said.

"You're too tired to put g's on the ends of your words," he said.

"You cook something," she said, feeling about to try to poke him. She missed and poked a cushion instead.

"We could order in."

"Plan good," she agreed.

"Or we could go out."

She opened her eyes and looked at him. "Ahem," he said, an exaggerated little cough. When she still didn't catch on, he extended his leg and held it out in front of her. She turned to survey it and screamed.

"You got it off."

"I got it off," he confirmed.

"You got it off," she screamed again, louder this time, as she propelled herself at him. He caught her and pulled her close. She hugged his neck, squealing, and he returned it, squeezing hard. "We have to go out."

"Of course we do, but of course we can't," he said.

She sat back to see his face. "Why not?"

"Um, hello, I saw you on the news twice today."

"I was only in the background," she said.

"Still, people are talking about you. There's chatter. You're sort of recognizable now. You can't be seen with me. I'm sullied goods."

"Yes, but you're *my* sullied goods, and you're officially free. It's too good, we have to get you out of this house. It's starting to become a little too *Rear Window* in here. You're about five days from gluing eyes on the silverware and pretending they're friends."

"I did that weeks before I met you, but then they back talked and I had to destroy them. What do you suggest? Do you want me to call your mom, ask if we can come over? Maybe she'll cook for us. Or we could try my mom, see if she might drop dead from a heart attack like my grandma. I should probably know if that kind of thing is hereditary," he said.

"I have an idea, come with me." She took his hand and tugged him to her house where she rooted in her brother's closet until she found what she was looking for.

"No," he said.

"Come on, Julian. You need a disguise, this is a disguise."

"It's a Sonny Bono costume," he said.

"I know. My sister was Cher. It was awkward and questionable when they won that karaoke competition. But for tonight, this is perfect for you. At least try it on." She stood on her toes and secured the wig and fake moustache on him.

"I look like Freddy Mercury," he said.

"Wow," Bronwyn breathed. "That's really…you look good."

"You are such a bad liar, but I am desperate enough to take it."

"A hat will help. Here." she held a baseball cap aloft for him.

He scowled. "You expect me to wear a baseball cap emblazoned with the NRA? Why don't I just dump blood on my head?"

"What? It's the last thing anyone would expect Julian Baxter to wear," she said.

"That's because he won't," he said.

She rolled her eyes. "Such a drama queen, Mr. Mercury. Fine, try one of these." She sifted in her brother's closet and came up with two more caps, one for Ford and one for John Deere.

"I'll take the John Deere," he said, reluctantly reaching for it. "It feels more like solidarity with my vegan friends."

"You might as well complete the ensemble," she said, handing him one of her brother's flannel shirts to layer over his trendy t-shirt.

He surveyed himself in the mirror. "Oh, geez. I look like I'm about to go propose to my cousin."

"She'd be lucky to have you," Bronwyn said, patting his arm. "Now let's go."

He put out a hand, holding her back. "We'll take my car," he said.

"You have a car?"

He gave her a slow smile. "Do I have a car?"

"Isn't that what I just said?"

"Let me show you my car," he said, leading the way back to his house and garage.

"It's a bit conspicuous," Bronwyn said, staring at the shiny red sports car.

"Yes, it is, Porsches are supposed to be," Julian said, bending over to press his face lovingly to the hood. He stood upright, fished his keys from his pocket and handed them to her.

"What?" she said, not understanding.

"I'm not allowed to drive because of all the DUI's. My license is suspended for another eighteen months."

She put her hands on her hips. "You drove drunk?"

"Many, many, many, too many to count, times. And I got caught five of those times, hence I have no license."

"That's abominable on so many levels," she said.

"Maybe your mom can work on toughening the penalties for repeat offenders while my mom can work on securing public funding for rehab. In the meantime, let's you and me get some grub." He pressed his keys into her palm and pointed her toward the driver's seat.

"Okay, but I...so plush," she said, scooting back and forth in the seat. She sniffed. "Is that real leather?"

"Don't tell my vegan friends," he said, adjusting his cap.

"You want to know what's unfair?" she asked.

"Everything?" he guessed.

"Yes, but I had a specific whine in mind this time. I have worked every day since college. I spent five years in a job I hated doing who knows what for mediocre pay, and all I have to show for it is a decrepit sedan that was already used when I bought it. You have done no work ever, wasted half your life being drunk or high, and have this hundred thousand dollar sports car."

"You know what the solution is, don't you?" he asked.

"Clearly not," she said.

"If we combine our lives, we get all the benefit of your worker bee ethic plus my debauched entitlement with none of the repercussions," he said.

"We've kind of already done that," she said.

"See? Together we're perfect," he said.

"I don't think..." she began, but he touched his fingers to her lips.

"Shh, together we're perfect."

She laughed. "Okay, together we're perfect."

They arrived at the restaurant and Bronwyn put in her name to be seated. People looked at them curiously, but neither knew if it was because Bronwyn was becoming recognizable or because Julian looked like a reject extra from the *Dukes of Hazzard.*

Julian was uncharacteristically quiet while they waited and even quieter after they were seated and placed their order.

"Is it hard to be in public again?" Bronwyn guessed.

"No."

"Do you feel weird being in disguise?" she tried.

"Only because the disguise is so heinous," he said. His eyes scanned the interior of the restaurant with a pinched, painful expression.

She took his hand and gave it a squeeze. "Julian, what's wrong?"

He took a shaky breath. "It's the booze."

She blinked at him, surprised. She wasn't drinking, and she hadn't thought anything of the alcohol around them.

"I can see it and, worse, I can smell it, and sometimes it's really hard because I still crave it. All the time, incessantly."

"I had no idea," she said.

"When I first got clean, I had a sober coach who went with me everywhere. Basically a babysitter who made sure I made it through those first torturous weeks. When I got busted for the probation violation and put on house arrest, it was kind of a relief. There's no alcohol in my parents' house, not even cough syrup, rubbing alcohol, or paint thinner because, yes, I would have used those. So I've been clean for eighteen months, and I'm ecstatic over my progress, but I also haven't faced a lot of temptation on my own."

"Julian, you're not on your own." She gave his hand a squeeze. "I'm here for whatever you need. Would you like to leave?"

"No, the more I face it and emerge triumphant, the stronger I'll be. It's like muscle memory, I have to practice."

"How can I best help you?"

"Being with me helps. The fact that you're not drinking helps. Otherwise, I need to keep my mind busy and distracted."

"Did someone order a distraction? I'm aces at those," she said and launched into a series of questions about him that kept up a stream of incessant, unending conversation for the next two hours, until long after their meal was finished and they'd ordered coffee. They were about to leave when a new table of men arrived next to them and ordered multiple beers and two bottles of wine. They were already sloppy drunk, loud, and obnoxious, but Julian looked at them longingly.

"I have one final question for you," Bronwyn said, tapping his hand to get his attention.

"What?" he asked, drawing his focus on her with effort.

"What was your first kiss?" she asked.

He looked at the ceiling, thinking. "I was twelve. She was fifteen and a senator's daughter. She was crazy hot, and I was the envy of all my friends. What was yours?"

"I was sixteen and sitting alone at the back of my property when the neighbor kid popped over the hedge and kissed me," she said.

He blinked at her, momentarily speechless. "I was your first kiss?"

She nodded. "And I'm kind of mad at you about it." She leaned in.

He did, too, and they made a cozy tableau, both bent over the table, their heads together. "Why? Because I did it without permission?"

"No. Because it was such a good kiss I spent a long time after being disappointed, thinking I would never find another that measured up."

"And when did you find one that measured up?" he asked.

She crooked a finger at him. He leaned in impossibly farther until she could whisper in his ear. "If it ever happens, I'll let you know."

# CHAPTER 18

For the next few weeks, Julian and Bronwyn practiced going out while maintaining his sobriety. He introduced her to his go-to sober drink: seltzer.

"It's terrible," she declared.

"You have to put lots of lemons in it. It's the only thing that makes it palatable."

She loaded the drink with lemons, found it was, indeed, palatable, and it became her standard drink, too. "For solidarity," she said, clinking her glass to his.

It helped him immensely to have her support, both spoken and unspoken, and he started going out without her occasionally, meeting friends for coffee in places he knew there was no alcohol until, eventually, he was able to get together with friends a couple of times at a place where alcohol was served. It was hard but not impossible, as long as he remembered to take it one day at a time, one moment at a time.

His lawyer finagled things to get his license back, and he was truly untethered.

"I guess you'll go back to DC now," Bronwyn said one night when they sat on his couch. Even though they could go out, they still spent a lot of time the same way they had before, at his house eating meals of their creation and then binging on television while he knitted. She sounded so sad, so forlorn at the prospect he smiled.

"And miss my little butterfly's metamorphosis? Never," he declared, and she hugged him around the neck and kissed his cheek.

Bronwyn was becoming buzzworthy, at least in the tight political circles that made up their combined world. Her mother's campaign had edged up three points, and more than a few people attributed that number to Bronwyn, whose appearance had added a much-needed shot of energy and enthusiasm, especially when it came to the much-coveted youth vote.

The first thing people noticed were the water bottles. Everyone in the campaign had the same one and used them incessantly, eschewing all plastic. First it became something of a joke, the conservative candidate trying to do the world a favor by drinking from a flask. But when everyone in the campaign and Laurel's entire family got on board with the commitment to renewables, it became an actual story, one that circulated in every major outlet and on the cover of a couple of magazines. No matter how much the more liberal outlets lampooned her, none of them could find a chink in her newfound commitment and, as Bronwyn had predicted, that authenticity went a long way with young voters.

Laurel herself seemed to have caught the new energy and enthusiasm and had started putting more of her own stuff on social media. She had a flair for self-deprecation and ended up being a big hit on Twitter and Instagram, even going so far as to make a little looped video of herself wagging her finger, a spoofed response to critics who said she was too hardline.

One day Bronwyn let herself into Julian's house. "Guess what? Carlo had a last minute..." her words faded and died. Julian sat at his kitchen table, a woman sat beside him, and it was someone Bronwyn recognized. In fact everyone in the country probably recognized her because she was a famous movie star. "Oh, sorry. I didn't know you had company."

Surprisingly, the woman also seemed to know her. Like many starlets, she had no trouble making her political opinions known, and many of those harsh opinions had been directed at Bronwyn's mother. "What is she doing here?" Her name was Georgiana Gaines, but everyone called her Gigi.

"Bronwyn's a friend of mine," Julian said. He gave her a smile that looked a bit strained.

"Why?" Gigi asked. "Do you know who her mother is, what she believes in?"

"Yes, but we are not our mothers," Julian said. He snapped his fingers at Bronwyn. "New motto, take note. We'll have it printed on matching t-shirts."

Bronwyn laughed, and the sound seemed to grate on Gigi's anger button.

"Julian, I can't even with her, really," she said. "You've been out here in the middle of nowhere too long if you're this hard up for entertainment."

"Gigi, let's not. We can have other friends," Julian said.

"Is that all we are, friends?" she had the tone, the possessive/flirtatious tone that spoke of a claim on Julian, on Bronwyn's Julian. He had never mentioned her, and she wondered why.

"Yes, you made that clear when you dumped me, remember?" he said.

*Oh,* Bronwyn thought, *that's why.* She hadn't previously kept up on his life enough to know who he dated, though she knew he often hobnobbed with celebrities. Now she felt conflicted—should she stay or should she go? The wine was the deciding factor. A full bottle of it sat on the table, and Bronwyn knew it had to have arrived with Gigi.

"What's the wine for?" she asked, sitting at the table uninvited beside Julian.

"To drink," Gigi said. "Do puritans not drink?"

"Not when their friends are alcoholics," Bronwyn said.

Gigi looked at Julian with big eyes and a fake expression of remorse. "Oh, no, I forgot. I'm so sorry."

She hadn't forgotten, Bronwyn knew. While she could easily forgive her for hating her mother and disagreeing with every one of her political beliefs, she could never forgive her for the blatant attempt to try and lure Julian back to alcohol. What kind of person did that? Had she brought drugs into the house, too? Julian had been doing so well, had been so strong in the face of the recent temptations he had faced by resuming life in public. And now this so-called friend had brought temptation into his home, flaunting it under his nose. It wasn't fair, it wasn't right. It was infuriating, and Bronwyn was properly furious.

"Can I ask you a question?" Gigi said.

"Sure," Bronwyn said, wary of her newly friendly tone.

"Are your parents actually brother and sister? Because the rumor is they are, and you and your siblings all seem inbred, so…" She shrugged.

"Gigi, stop," Julian said. "You came all this way to visit. Is this how you want to spend it?"

"Exactly, Julian, I came all this way to visit *you*, not this…" she said a word then, a word no one had ever used to describe Bronwyn, at least not to her face.

There were a few beats of shocked silence, and then Julian spoke. His voice was low and angry and dangerous.

"You can't say that about Bronwyn."

"Are you really serious with this?" Gigi asked, motioning to Bronwyn.

"Yes. If you can't be civil to her, then get out."

Gigi blinked at him. "What, are you, like, lovers or something?" she gave an uncomfortable half laugh as if the thought was unfathomable to her.

"What we are is none of your business. We broke up, remember?" Julian said.

Gigi looked at Bronwyn, and it was clear she was having some kind of internal debate with herself. At last she stood. "I can't. I can't be in the same room with this trash." A few seconds later they heard the front door slam, and then a car roared to life.

"I…" Julian began, but Bronwyn held up a hand.

"Hold on." She took the bottle of wine, bashed it against the sink until the top broke off, and then turned on the water to wash it down. When the scent still lingered, she pulled bleach from beneath the sink and sloshed a generous amount down the drain, chasing the smell.

"That was an eight hundred dollar bottle of wine," Julian informed her.

"And now it's a heap of bleached trash." She bagged it twice and tossed it in the bin. When that was finished, she resumed her seat at the table beside Julian.

"Thank you," he said.

"No, thank you. It was nice the way you stood up for me with her. I'm sorry you had to."

"It's not your fault," he said.

"No one from your side has ever talked to me like that in person before," she said. "It was brutal, almost like a physical punch."

"A few years ago, when my mom got in a car accident, some people from your side sent me personal messages saying they hoped she was dead, and they hoped I died on the way to the hospital to see her."

Bronwyn winced. "That's horrifying. When did we lose our humanity?"

"I don't know, but I'd like to get it back."

"For the record, I have disagreed vehemently with your side before, but I have never gone outside the lines, never spoken to anyone like that, never wished anyone dead," Bronwyn said.

"I know you haven't. That's what makes you one of the good ones," he said. "And while I can't vouch for the dark years when I wasn't myself, I've never done anything like that in the years before or since. Although, occasionally I do like to tease."

"I hadn't noticed," she said dryly.

"Oh, come on. You all make it so easy with the gun thing and the macho guy/subservient woman routine."

"Julian," she warned.

"Right, you're right, I see where this is heading. I promise to try to be kind to everyone from your side, even when we disagree."

"Me too," she said.

"It sort of feels like we're saying a vow," he said.

"Yes."

"If only there were some way to seal it. Think, Bronwyn, think." He reached for her, pulling her into his lap.

She ran her fingers through his hair. "We could, I don't know, swap spit."

"Yes, I'm all in for that," he said.

She brought her hand to her mouth, but he caught it.

"You're about to spit into your hand, aren't you?" he asked.

"Isn't that how it's done? We spit in our hands and shake on it? Otherwise, I'm not sure what you had in mind," she said.

"If you spit, I will disown and banish you forever," he said.

"Well, I'm not taking any chances on that," she said. "What if we kiss on it?"

He nodded.

She kissed his cheek.

"Out, get out of my house," he said, attempting to stand and push her off.

"I cling like a barnacle," she informed him, wrapping her arms and legs around him in a death grip so he was forced to sit back down. He didn't have to wrap his arms around her to keep her there, but he did.

"You're a rotten kid," he said, their faces now a centimeter apart. "What am I going to do with you?"

"I have an idea," she said.

"Is this another trick?" he asked.

"No, this is serious. Come away with me this weekend."

He blinked at her. "What?"

"I have to go away this weekend, and I want you to go with me," she said.

"What about Carlo?"

"I asked Carlo, and he can't get away from work."

"I'm feeling very confused about your perception of my interchangeability with your boyfriend," he said.

"First of all, he's not my boyfriend."

"Bronwyn, come on. You guys have been dating each other exclusively for weeks now."

"That may be true, but he's never said the words, and I won't be the first to use them," she said. "Second, my mom has to have a root canal."

He pushed her away, putting some distance between them, though she remained on his lap. "Start from the beginning."

"My mom has to have a root canal and can't do her stump speech this weekend. She and Jeffrey asked me to go in her place."

He grasped her biceps. "You've been called up to the big leagues?"

She nodded, trying and failing not to look as pleased as she felt.

"This is huge," Julian said.

"It is, and I want you there beside me," she said. "In fact, I'm not certain I can do it without you."

"I'm positive you can, and I would love to go, but Bronwyn, how? There is no way I can spend an entire weekend as Sonny Bono. No one is going to buy that getup up close."

"Of course not, which is why I bought you a better, more believable costume," she said.

"Another costume? You do realize we're not in an episode of *Saved by the Bell,* don't you? These crazy schemes of yours are sitcom gold. How stupid do you think people are?"

"Stupid, really, really stupid. I think people see what they want and they look for the most obvious answer. If someone sees you with me, they may wonder who you are, but they will never in a million years think you're Julian Baxter. Look, one time when I was little we went to Disneyworld. It was right after the first election and my mom was really famous for unseating an incumbent,"

"My mom," he interjected.

"Right, that's the one. Anyway, she'd been all over the news and in tons of shows. So we went to Disneyworld and a few people stopped and looked. Finally one guy came up to her and said, 'Do you know who you look like? That conservative chick who just got elected to Congress. You're prettier, though. She's kind of severe.' It became this big family joke, and it's happened tons of times since then. Nobody ever expects to see someone they don't expect to see so they end up not actually seeing that person, you know?"

"I kind of think I do, and I'm scared we're close enough now for me to follow that kind of logic."

"Please, Julian, please? I'll be your best friend," she said, clutching her hands together under his chin and resting her head on his shoulder.

"And if I say no?"

"I'll still be your best friend, but I'll be a little disappointed," she said.

"We can't have that," he said. "Show me the costume."

"You're going to hate it," she promised.

"Indubitably," he agreed, and they went to try it on.

# CHAPTER 19

Bronwyn was having more fun than she thought humanly possible. She was back at the place where she was born in rural Virginia, the place where she spent the first few years of her life, among old acquaintances who knew her family well, in the small town where her parents had spent the early part of their marriage before her mother got elected. Being back made her feel nostalgic for the way things were before her mother became obsessed with politics. Back then they had been a normal family, if larger than some. The memories were sweet. Whether they were real or Bronwyn was viewing them through a hazy lens of longing, she had no idea. And she didn't much care. All she knew was she felt as if she were reconnecting with her roots, and it confirmed a part of her identity she hadn't been able to pinpoint. She was not Bronwyn Porter, political power daughter from Washington, DC. She was Bronwyn Porter, homespun small town girl.

The fly in the ointment, as always, was her mother. Even while doped up on pain meds after her root canal, she was attempting to control Bronwyn vicariously over the phone.

"What are you wearing?" had been her mother's opening sentence during the first call.

"A sweater and jeans. Don't worry, I'm planning to change before the speech," Bronwyn assured her.

"Not that, I meant what is on your head?"

Bronwyn looked up, going cross eyed at the attempt to see the hat Julian had made for her. It was October, and the weather had turned nippy. He had presented her with the hat and matching gloves at the start of their trip. "For luck," he said.

"It's a hat," Bronwyn said.

"I can see it's a hat," Laurel replied.

Bronwyn spun in a quick circle. "How can you see?" Was her mother staked out in a high-rise hotel somewhere with a scope, *a la* Lee Harvey Oswald?

"Someone sent me a picture because it's ridiculous. Take it off."

Now Bronwyn turned to scowl at her entourage. She supposed it was too much they be loyal to her when they worked for her mother, but still. The betrayal stung. "No."

"Why not? Are you purposely trying to look like a fool?" her mother asked.

"Mom, my very good friend made me this hat and these mittens, and I happen to love them. I'm not taking them off."

"How old is your friend and is she blind and incapable of using her fingers?" Laurel countered.

"Circles are hard to knit," Bronwyn snapped. It was Julian's first attempt at doing anything other than a straight stitch, so of course it was a little sloppy. But Bronwyn didn't care; she loved them, even more so knowing how much it annoyed her mother.

"Take it off, Bronwyn."

"Mom, it's really hard to take you seriously when you can't say your R's properly," Bronwyn said. Her mother was clearly still numb and probably packed with some kind of cotton.

"Stop being stubborn and take off the hat. Trust me, I know what I'm saying. I've done this a time or two," Laurel said. Her tone was imperious, but it was ruined when it came out sounding like "twust me."

"Going to have to pry the mittens off my cold, dead corpse, Mom.

They're staying. I don't care how they look, they're meaningful to me. And I'm not here for photo ops, I'm here to talk to people, real people."

"Real people still have eyes and cameras," her mother countered.

"Then I'll smile pretty so they can get a great big shot of my face," Bronwyn promised. "Got to go, I'm here." She didn't say where exactly, but it didn't matter. She had to get off the phone with her mother or risk developing an eye twitch.

"Your mom's a big fan of my work, I take it," Julian said.

"She doesn't like things that are homemade," Bronwyn informed him. "Which is ironic, considering she made a lot of our clothes back when we were poor. Our first few family photos look like the country version of the Von Trapp children with matching trout-printed jumpsuits."

"Trout?"

"My dad's big into fly fishing."

"It's almost like she knows the hat's from me and hates it preemptively," he said, sounding somewhat sad.

Bronwyn had to resist the urge to reach out and comfort him. She wasn't sure which the press would deem worse, being seen hugging Julian or being seen holding the hand of the apparently paunchy middle aged guy Julian was pretending to be. The costume had said, "Dad Bod," and was as horrifying in real life as it had looked on the internet. He now sported a paunchy gut and a long mullet, in addition to another moustache, one less inspiring than the Sonny Bono/Freddy Mercury one he'd worn before. She wasn't sure how it was possible for someone as dashingly handsome as Julian to look dowdy, but somehow the America Costume Company had made it happen.

"You're still my favorite," she said, in lieu of a hug.

"Finding you adorable when I look like this makes me feel like a creepy old dude," he said.

"What do you think it's doing to me to find you adorable right now?" she asked.

"We need therapy."

"Lots and lots."

"What do you think everyone else thinks of the little friendship you have going with the random middle aged photographer who follows you around?" he said.

"That I have daddy issues?" she guessed.

"I bet if I dressed like your mom instead, our future therapists could get a paper published about it," he said.

"Still not worth it," she said, grimacing.

"Definitely not," he agreed. He opened the door for her, and they entered the nursing home side by side. It had been Bronwyn's idea to visit the nursing home. Initially she was only supposed to meet with some farmers and local business owners, but she had opted to add in a school visit, as well as the nursing home, in keeping with their commitment to cradle-to-grave pro-life efforts. It wasn't a big voting bloc, and certainly not their key demographic, but Bronwyn was trying to look at the big picture, to keep her focus on caring for people and remaining authentic.

It was a small nursing home, and she was able to visit with everyone who was coherent enough to talk and shake hands. One lady in particular was taken with her mittens and hat.

"These look handmade," she said.

"Yes, they are."

"You knit? So few young people today do," the woman said.

"That's true, and I'm one of the unfortunate ones who doesn't. My friend made these for me, and he's young."

"A young man who knits? Sounds like a keeper," the woman said.

"I think so," Bronwyn agreed, tossing Julian a smile.

After the nursing home, they had lunch at a local hot dog joint, along with the town's mayor. Bronwyn and Julian didn't sit together, but he texted her a couple of times. And she answered surreptitiously, under the table.

*You're killing it,* he said at one point.

*Thanks,* she replied.

*I'm serious. You're really, really good at this.*

*You're biased,* she said.

*True, but I've been around this stuff my whole life, and you have the knack. Want to know how much? You've almost convinced ME to vote for your mother.*

She had snickered at that and then tried to pretend she was laughing at the mayor's boring story.

The most uncomfortable part of the visit, at least for Bronwyn, was when talk turned to Evelyn Baxter, Julian's mother. Both the tone and the words were vitriolic, shockingly so. Had it always been that way, or was Bronwyn sensitized to it because Julian was nearby listening?

*I shouldn't have dragged you along,* Bronwyn texted him at one point.

*I wanted to come,* he replied. *Seeing you in action has been fun, and it's kind of hot to be clandestine, like spies.*

*They're dragging your mom, worse than I imagined. I didn't think about how you would feel. Selfish.*

*I'm a politician's kid, skin like a rhino. I'm fine, stop worrying.*

Despite his reassurances, she didn't stop worrying about it. And she felt awkward and vaguely guilty and ashamed. It wasn't her place to correct strangers, was it? When she was supposed to be stumping for her mother, it seemed unwise to stick up for her opponent. On the other hand, the tone of so many people she talked to bordered on the psychotic, as if they thought Evelyn Baxter would be personally responsible for the total collapse of society if she got elected.

By the time her speech rolled around, Bronwyn felt shaken and vaguely ill about the whole situation. Julian, on the other hand, was as supportive and encouraging as ever. He hovered sedately in the background, absorbing the harsh words about his mother with barely a flicker of expression. But that only increased Bronwyn's worry and guilt. He had come on this trip for her. Didn't she owe him more than complacent silence?

She was still puzzling over the dilemma when her mother called.

"Stick to the script."

"I know, Mom. You told me already."

"Yes, Bronwyn, but so far you haven't been doing a good job of following my instructions," Laurel said.

"I haven't been doing a good job, or I haven't been following your instructions?" Bronwyn clarified, and Julian gave her a thumb's up.

"They're not mutually exclusive. You're good with people, I'll give you that."

"Thank you, your majesty," Julian whispered. Bronwyn covered his mouth, and he licked her palm. She was busy wiping her hand on his shirt when her mother continued.

"But this is a speech. You have no experience public speaking."

"That's not true, I took a class in high school," Bronwyn countered.

"And what happened?" Laurel prompted.

"I blacked out and hit my head on a desk," Bronwyn said. "Thank you for helping me relive the memory, Mom, I had almost forgotten. But after that I did all right in that class."

"It's different speaking in front of a huge group of people and live reporters. One wrong move, and this will be piped to everyone in creation for all of eternity," Laurel warned.

"Mom, I'm seriously going to puke. Why are you purposely trying to freak me out?"

"I'm not trying to freak you out, I'm trying to make you realize this is serious and you need to stick to the script."

"What makes you think I won't?" Bronwyn asked.

"Twenty seven years of experience as your mother," Laurel said, and Julian gave Bronwyn a silent high five.

"I have to go. It's almost time," Bronwyn said. "Do you have anything constructive to say?"

"Don't black out," Laurel replied and, unable to take it anymore, Julian ripped the phone out of Bronwyn's fingers and ended the call.

"So, what are you going to do?" he asked.

"I'm going to stick to the script. Right? I mean, she was pretty clear on that, and it's not like I know anything about writing speeches."

"No, but you know your heart, you know this town, you know these people. If you think the speech is on point, then by all means go with it. But I get the sense you don't believe that, so I think you should trust your gut and follow your heart. You have good instincts and an even better heart." He kissed her forehead and pointed her toward the stage.

Bronwyn walked up to the podium and checked her notes. The speech was supposed to be a reiteration of her mother's policy, especially as it related to crime and the economy. But when Bronwyn opened her mouth, it was as if something else took over and she didn't read the words on the page. Instead she did as Julian said and tried to speak from the heart.

"Thank you all for hosting me today. I've so enjoyed getting to know you, hearing your stories. Mostly I've enjoyed being back home. Even though I've lived in DC for much of my life, this has always felt more real to me, more connected to my family.

"I've heard a lot of talk since I've been here about defeating our enemy, Evelyn Baxter."

There were boos. Bronwyn held up her hand, smiling. "I'm here to tell you today Evelyn Baxter is not our enemy. She's an intelligent, capable, highly accomplished woman. She deserves our applause, and not our censure."

The audience hushed, not sure of what to do.

"I'm a lifelong conservative." She held a little square of paper aloft. "This is my membership card to the NRA. I've had it since I was fifteen though, to be honest, I've never fired a gun. But I do believe in the Second Amendment, in our right to bear arms."

There was more applause. Bronwyn waited it out before speaking again. "I've grown up in one of the most prominently conservative families in the country. My very best friend is a lifelong liberal, a massive supporter of the ACLU who believes strongly in socialized healthcare." There were a few boos at that. She waited them out. "But I'm here to tell you I couldn't survive one day on this planet without him. I don't care what he does in the voting booth; I care what he does outside it. I care that he's a kind, compassionate man of deep integrity.

"Friends, Evelyn Baxter is *not* our enemy. Poverty is our enemy. Joblessness is our enemy. Crime is our enemy. The corruption of government institutions is our enemy. The breakdown of the family is our enemy. My mother has ideas about how to help fix these things, and I believe they're good ideas. Evelyn Baxter has ideas about how to fix these things, and that's where we part ways and disagree. But let's not get caught up believing any of our fellow citizens are against us when we're all working toward one common purpose: to make our nation greater.

"On election day, you have a choice to make. If you choose to believe, like I do, my mother's policies will help fix our country, then please vote for her. If you believe Evelyn Baxter's policies will help fix our country, then please vote for her. Either way, let's not fall into the trap of believing our politics define us. People come first, always. Politics, well, that's just a bunch of chatter. So when you leave that booth on voting day, love your neighbor. Say hello. Check on them. And if they have a need, be the one to meet it. Thank you for having me today." She gave a little wave, and they applauded her off the stage. The applause was subdued, almost stunned.

She reached Julian, her hands shaking. He picked her up and held her close, his lips close to her ear. "It was perfect, I loved it. Thank you."

"I don't know," she said uncertainly. "I don't think they liked it. Maybe I should have stuck to the script."

"The script was rubbish. That speech you gave was inspired. And by the way, it's mutual. I don't see myself surviving a minute here without you, either."

Her arms circled his neck. "How do you know I was talking about you?"

"You have a lot of liberal best friends?" he asked, smiling.

"Scads of them," she said. "I'm immensely popular, always have been."

"Popularity is overrated. True friendship is not," he said.

"You got that off a fortune cookie, didn't you?" she asked.

"Inspirational cat poster," he corrected.

Her phone rang, and he set her down. "It's my brother," she whispered.

"Which one?" he asked.

"Scott, the oldest."

"The scariest," he whispered, shuddering.

"Thanks, that's helpful." He grasped her hand and gave it a squeeze as she pushed the button to answer. "Hello."

"Bronwyn, it's Scott."

"I know. I have this new thing Caller ID. I think it might take off. Might want to invest, get in on the ground floor."

"What?" Her brother had never gotten her sense of humor, like everyone else in her family. To make matters worse, she tended to blather incoherently when she was nervous. Julian gave her hand an encouraging squeeze. She took a deep breath.

"Nothing, what's up? Did Mom tell you to call me?" She gripped the phone, bracing herself for an indirect lecture. Her mother had occasionally used her siblings to hand down vicarious directives.

"No. This isn't coming from Mom, it's coming from me. I watched your speech."

She squeezed her eyes closed. "Yes."

"I thought it was brilliant. Who wrote that?"

"I did," she squeaked.

"I thought so. I loved it, so genuine, so on point. It reminded me of Mom, in the early days, before she went bat crap crazy."

"You think Mom is crazy?" she asked. Her eyes flew to Julian who gave her a thumb's up and smile.

He chuckled. "Yes, Bronwyn. We all think Mom is crazy. But we're all too scared of her to say so."

"How long has everyone thought that?" she asked.

"Since she got elected the first time and, well, went crazy. Remember what it was like before?" His tone held the same nostalgia she felt every time she thought of their life before.

"Yes." She sniffled, pressing back her ever-ready tears. "How's life in the navy?"

"Less structured than life under Mom," he said, and Bronwyn laughed. They talked a few more minutes, catching up on their siblings, and then disconnected.

"You doing all right?" Julian asked when she set aside the phone and continued to stare into space.

"I don't know. I waited so long for something like that, for some recognition of my existence from someone in my family, for some scrap of approval. To have it now feels a bit redundant."

"Why redundant?" Julian asked.

"Because I already have it from you," she said. Their eyes caught and held. Bronwyn felt a flush creep up her cheeks. His hand reached out and pushed a strand of hair off her face.

"Bronwyn," he whispered.

"Yes?"

"Your phone is ringing again."

She jumped to attention and tensed as she recognized her mother's ring. "You don't have to take it," Julian said.

"Best to get it over with," she said. Taking another bracing breath, she picked up the phone. "Hello."

There was silence for a few beats, and Bronwyn tensed. Silence with her mother was usually ominous. This time, however, she seemed to be searching for the proper words.

"I'm not happy," Laurel began slowly.

"Mom..."

"However, Jeffrey was here watching the speech with me, and we both agreed it was pretty good. The high road looks good on us, people have been responding to it. So I guess it turned out okay."

*Just okay?* Bronwyn wanted to press, but she didn't. Maybe things with her mother needed to heal in tiny doses. And maybe it was time for her to give a dose, too. "I learned from the best, Mom."

"You really did," Laurel said, and Bronwyn laughed. Her mom could be funny, when she wanted. "See you on Monday."

"See you," Bronwyn replied.

"She liked it," Julian guessed.

"I think so," Bronwyn said, wonder in her tone.

"It must feel like waking up to realize you've won the lottery, but it was twenty seven years ago and you could have been celebrating all this time," he said.

"Julian," she said, a hint of frustration in her tone.

'What?" he asked, clueless as to how he could have upset her.

"You say things like that, and it makes me want to pelt myself at you, but I've already passed my limit of how many times I can hug the creepy old weirdo who follows me."

He picked her up and hugged her. "It's okay, I thought of a new story for us."

"What's that?" she asked, returning the hug.

"I'm your stalker."

"That only explains why you're hugging me, not why I'm hugging you," she said.

"You're desperate and psychotic," he said.

"Oh, goody. Thanks." She didn't actually care anymore, though. The weekend had been a success and the speech was going well. In her current mood, she believed nothing could go wrong. Soon she would remember the feeling and shake her head at her naiveté.

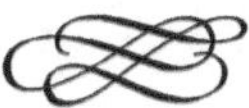

# CHAPTER 21

Bronwyn's team had been bugging her to go out with them for weeks, but she had been busy splitting her time between Carlo and Julian. Finally she found a night when both Carlo and Julian had other plans, and her team was taking her to a trendy pub-style restaurant in the city. They walked into the restaurant, and her phone buzzed with a text from Carlo. *Meetings all night. Ugh. Miss you.* She was just about to send him a reply when Todd spoke.

"Oh, no, look who's here."

"Baxter spawn," Cara supplied.

Bronwyn's head snapped up and saw Julian sitting across the room with a group of friends. One of his friends said something to him, pointed toward their group, and his head whipped in her direction. He tipped his drink to her, a seltzer, and she pressed her lips together to push back her smile.

"Ugh, let's go somewhere else," Todd said.

"No way," Bronwyn said. "It's a free country."

"Not if his mom gets elected," Cara replied.

"Let's put that away for tonight and have fun, okay?" Bronwyn suggested.

"Hating the Baxters is how I have fun," Cara replied.

Bronwyn gave her a look.

"Fine, but he better stay away," Cara muttered.

"You have a lot of anger," Todd said.

"Don't test me," Cara said.

"Never said I didn't like it," Todd countered.

They were seated, and Jonah spoke. "We should send him something."

Claire piped up. "I heard he's an alcoholic. Let's send him a drink."

"No," Bronwyn said, smacking her menu on the table so hard everyone jumped and looked at her. "We don't play like that. We take the high road, always. Besides, I know exactly what to send him, but someone's going to need to run next door to the bakery." Cara volunteered and returned a few minutes later, handing the item to Bronwyn.

"I don't get it, though," Claire said, and everyone nodded their agreement as they stared at the blueberry scone.

"Our families have been feuding for two decades. Believe me, he'll know what it means," Bronwyn assured her.

They gave it to the waitress and had it delivered as an omelet arrived for Bronwyn.

"An omelet? What does that mean?" Todd asked.

"I hate eggs," Bronwyn said.

"Oh," Cara drawled. "And they know that because they've mapped all your likes and dislikes. That's diabolical." She was serious, Bronwyn realized, and she couldn't stop a chuckle as she pushed the plate away and let everyone else eat the omelet. Her phone buzzed with a text from Julian.

*Your scones are better.*

*Your omelet is the same,* she replied. *Inedible.*

*You're cute,* he texted.

*You're cuter.*

*Not this again. You're going to wear out my battery,* he wrote.

*Time to get a new pacemaker, Grandpa.*

"Are you talking to Carlo?" Cara asked.

"Of course she is. She only gets that look when she's talking to Carlo," Claire added.

"What look?" Bronwyn said.

"Dreamy," Jonah said.

"Dude, are you a twelve year old girl? Don't say dreamy," Todd said.

"Unless you're using it ironically," Bronwyn agreed.

The restaurant became increasingly louder and more crowded. It was a trendy hotspot for up and comers of their age in DC, a place to see and be seen. Bronwyn had never actually been before and, while she enjoyed seeing several familiar faces and saying hello, the frenetic environment was giving her a headache. To make it worse, the table was out of lemons and their waitress was nowhere in sight. Eventually she gave up trying to track her down and went to the bar for more.

Once at the bar, however, she had no better luck with the bartender. He was busy and not paying attention to her Oliver Twist pose, bowl outstretched, pathetic expression. Someone walked up to her right side and deposited a few slices of lemon in her bowl.

"I couldn't help notice you're also drinking the seltzer, and it's no good without lemon," Julian said.

"Too true," Bronwyn said. "Thank you."

"Why a seltzer? Are you an alcoholic?" he asked, leaning on the bar.

"No, but my best friend is. Solidarity." She tipped the bowl to him in a little salute.

"I'm sure he appreciates that," he said. He squinted at her. "You look familiar. Do I know you from somewhere?"

"Prison?" she guessed.

"Wouldn't know. Thanks to rich privilege, I've never actually been," he said.

"Pro-life rally?" she guessed.

"Not my scene. Pride parade?" he countered.

"Never been. I heard you have to be gay to attend," she added in a stage whisper.

"Wait a minute, aren't you my neighbor?"

"Doesn't ring a bell," she said.

"No, I'm fairly certain. You play soccer, right?" he asked.

"No, that's my sister."

"Lacrosse?" he tried.

"Nope, other sister."

"Are you the one who stands by the hedge and sneaks cookies?" he said.

"Yes, that's me," she agreed.

"Oh, now I remember; you're the cute one. But I feel like I know you from somewhere else. Did we go to camp together?"

She narrowed her eyes at him. "Probably not. I went to a highly specialized camp for people with big glands."

His eyes skimmed her up and down. "I find that extremely difficult to believe. There's something else familiar about you." He shifted slightly closer. "Have my lips been on you?"

"That's possible. I'd venture to say your lips have been a lot of places," she said.

"I might need a refresher, to make certain it was you," he said.

"Sorry, I have a boyfriend."

"I bet he's dreamy." He glanced behind her. "Have you ever seen *West Side Story*?"

"Yes, why?"

"Because I think the Jets are on their way for a rumble," he said.

She turned and saw the rest of her group heading her direction, looking mutinous. "Play it cool, Riff," she whispered. "Hey, guys."

"Is he giving you trouble?" Todd asked, flexing. Julian snickered a laugh, and Todd's eyes narrowed.

"No, we were having a word," Bronwyn said.

"Are you kids on your way to church?" Julian asked. "Or is it Amish rumsrpinga time?"

Bronwyn faced him with a wrinkled nose. "Not cool," she mouthed.

"You want to take this outside?" Todd asked.

"No one is taking anything outside. Can you imagine the headline on that? I'll handle this," Bronwyn said, tapping a restraining hand on his chest.

She turned to face Julian again and straightened her dress before motioning him closer with her finger. He tipped his head to her. She stood on her toes, cupped her hands around his ear, and whispered. "Your mom."

"Geez," he said, laughing. "I concede. You win, so long as you never, ever say that again."

"That's what I thought. Take care, Baxter spawn," she said.

"Later, Maria," he said, tossing her a wink.

Bronwyn and her team turned to go. "If it was anyone but him, I'd say he was hitting on you," Cara said.

A minute later, Bronwyn received a text from Julian. She pulled it out and read, *She's not wrong.*

Smiling, she tucked her phone back in her purse.

few days later, Bronwyn was at work when someone tapped her on the shoulder. "Excuse me, ma'am, do you know where I can get some of them Laurel Portman signs for my yard?"

Bronwyn turned to face the man asking the question. "Sure, if you go to..." she stopped short, her mouth hanging open in shock. It was Julian, but not. If she weren't staring into his eyes and reading the mischief, she would have been fooled. "Come with me, I'll help you." She grasped his arm, marched him to a supply closet, glanced around to make sure no one was looking, and shoved him inside.

"Wow, I should have done this ages ago," he said, settling his hands at her waist.

"What are you doing here?" she hissed. "We're going to get caught."

"No way, this disguise is foolproof. One of my friends who's a makeup artist hooked me up."

"Seriously, what are you doing here?" she asked. It was a small space. Her arms had nowhere to go but around him.

"I really want some Laurel Portman yard signs. I'm thinking of having a bonfire. Also, I'm here to kidnap you."

"What?"

"Play hooky with me," he said, resting his forehead on hers.

"I can't do that."

"Why not?"

"Because I'm a responsible adult," she said.

"You have never skipped anything a day in your life, have you?" he asked.

"No."

"Then you're well overdue. Welcome to the Julian Baxter school of shirking responsibility, a master course. And don't use your mother as an excuse because I know she's not here today."

When she took a long time to answer, he knew she was having a debate with herself. She opened her mouth, and he preempted her.

"If you lecture me about being a contributing member of society again, I'm going to bite you," he warned.

Her arms tightened on him as a slow smile spread over her face. "It's important we give back, that we own up to our responsibilities and…oh."

He bit her earlobe. She clutched at him, out of necessity this time to keep from falling over. "Your inner ear again?" he whispered, his breath tickling the spot he'd just bitten.

"It's getting worse," she replied.

"You really should have that looked at." He kissed the earlobe. "Come out with me today, please."

She nodded, too undone for more speech.

"Excellent. I'm parked two blocks down the road. Meet me there in ten minutes."

She arrived on time, wearing oversized sunglasses and skulking like a cat burglar. "Were you followed?" he asked.

"No, but drive around the block a few times, in case," she said. Since he didn't know if she was joking and since he wouldn't put it past Laurel to have put a tail on her daughter, he did as she said.

"What do you want to do?" he asked.

"I thought you had a plan," she said.

"I did: show up at your job and steal you away. Ta-da."

"You know what I really want to do? I want to go home, swim, and watch a bunch of TV. I'm so exhausted from adulting all the time." She rested her head on the seat and closed her eyes.

He rested his hand on her leg and gave it a reassuring pat. "Sounds good."

"No it doesn't. It sounds pathetic. And you're finally free now. We should do something fabulous."

"To be honest, I don't want to. It's way too peopley out there today. I think all the months of confinement gave me borderline agoraphobia."

"Then by all means let's keep it going," she said.

"That's what best friends are for, to feed your mental illness," he said, and they bumped fists.

Julian parked in his garage and they walked to Bronwyn's house. They had no sooner let themselves in the back door when another car pulled up and someone opened the door. Julian hustled Bronwyn into the pantry.

"Twice in one day," she whispered, but he shushed her. She thought it was Louisa come to check on something, but a moment later she heard her mother's voice echoing loudly in the cavernous kitchen.

# CHAPTER 22

"I'm telling you she's not here," Laurel said.

"Are you certain?" Jeffrey replied.

Bronwyn tensed, frowning. Why was Jeffrey with her mother? Did they know she skipped work? Had she and Julian been followed? Was she about to be found out and fired? Before she could panic too much, Julian pressed his palms over her ears.

She glanced up at him, amused, but his look was serious, intent, almost pained.

"What?" she mouthed.

He shook his head, his lips pressed tightly together in a grimace.

She peeled his hands off her ears. It took effort because he resisted her. He shook his head at her. She was still half laughing, and then she realized what was going on. Conversation in the kitchen had come to a halt, but the noise hadn't. It was extremely obvious to her what was happening, and yet she couldn't believe it.

Her eyes flew back to Julian's, and the expression he gave her confirmed the worst. *Maybe it's not what I think. Maybe it's the TV. Maybe Jeffrey was only here for a second and left,* she thought. Shaking free of Julian's restraining grasp, she cracked the door open and peeked out, and then remained frozen, unable to decipher what her eyes saw. Jeffrey and her mother...her mother and Jeffrey...

Julian closed the door, turned her to face him, and pressed his palms back over her ears. This time she didn't resist. In fact she did nothing. She stared blankly at his chest and prayed for some kind of divine intervention.

A little while later he removed his hands from her ears and leaned in to whisper. "They went upstairs. Let's sneak out." He took her hand, pulled her behind him out of the house, over the hedge, and next door. Once there, he steered her to the entertainment room and pushed her into a sitting position on the couch. He sat beside her, but didn't touch her. For that she was glad. She didn't want to touch or be touched just then, didn't want to think or feel or know or remember. She wanted a mental fog to swallow her whole, to ward off all emotion and everything else.

"This is what you knew," she said.

"Yes."

"And you didn't tell me."

"No."

"How could you have kept this from me?"

"How could I have told you?" he countered. "How could I be the one to disillusion you, to impart this kind of earth shattering revelation?"

"How can you call yourself my friend and go on allowing me to live in such ignorance?" She stood.

"Bronwyn, where are you going?"

"I'm leaving." She stormed out of the room. He didn't follow. A few minutes later she came back and sat down again. "I have nowhere to go." She sighed. "I'm sorry, I'm not actually mad at you."

"I know. Please don't apologize. I'm the one who's sorry. For everything."

"How long?" she asked. How long had her mother been a traitor to everything she believed, to everything she stood for? To their entire family?

"I've known for five years. I have no idea if it was going on before then."

"Have there been others?"

"Do you really want to know?" he asked.

"No."

"Are you doing all right?" he asked.

"Yes," she answered, then stood and darted for the bathroom where she promptly lost her lunch in the toilet. Julian entered and rested his hand on her back. With his other hand, he gathered her hair and held it while she got sick again and again until there was nothing left. She had never thrown up in front of anyone but her mother and Louisa before, but she was too spent to care.

Julian flushed the toilet a couple of times, retrieved a cool cloth for her forehead, and led her down the hall to the guest room. He sat her down, pulled off her shoes, and pushed her back. When she was lying down, he took off his own shoes and climbed into the big bed beside her. He propped his elbow and rested his head in his hand, studying her.

"Are you going to cry now or are you going to cry later?" he asked.

"Probably both. And I'm a really ugly crier."

"Me too," he assured her.

She smiled. Julian skimmed his finger over her face as they stared at each other. She didn't want to cry. If she cried, she would have to think, to feel. "You should sleep," he suggested. "Second to alcohol and drugs, sleep is my favorite escape from reality. Bonus: it's non-addictive."

"I'm not sure I can sleep with someone staring at me," she said.

"You do it every night," he said then, realizing she thought he was serious, rolled his eyes. "Joking. Here." He pulled her toward him, cuddling her against him with her face to his chest, his arm over his waist. "Better?" His fingers eased through the ends of her hair, caressing gently against her back.

"Yes," she said. Even if she didn't fall asleep, it was immensely comforting to be held. That was her last thought before she slipped blissfully into unconsciousness.

She woke an unknown time later, still foggy and half asleep. Julian's solid presence was still beside her, only now her head was on his chest, his arm around her. She took a deep breath and froze. The person beside her was not Julian. The smell wasn't the same; the feel of him was different. In her confusion, she felt a moment of panic. Who had sneaked in to replace Julian? Where was he? Was he okay?

Bracing herself to face a burglar, she opened her eyes and saw Carlo staring at her with a concerned smile. "Hi, *querida.*"

"Hi," she said, still more than a little confused. If she blurted, *What are you doing here,* it would sound like an unfriendly accusation, as if she didn't want him there. But of course she wanted him there, he was her...fella. It was just that she had expected Julian. "How did you know I was here?" she tried instead.

"Work said you left early. You didn't answer your phone, so I tried Julian. He said you were here sleeping off a headache."

"Oh," she said. She sat up and drew her knees to her chest, wrapping her arms around them. Everything came speeding back to her, the reason she was there. She swallowed hard, pushing back the emotion, shoving it down somewhere deep.

Carlo sat up beside her. "Bronwyn, is everything okay?"

"Yes," she said, but there was no way he could believe her. Even a stranger could see she was upset.

"Is it your mother?" he asked, pushing her hair off her shoulder and letting his fingers linger soothingly on her tight, tense muscles.

She blinked at him. Did he know about her mother? Did everyone know but her? Did her father know? Her brothers and sisters?

"Did she say something to upset you?" he clarified.

"What would make you think that?" she asked.

"Because you're only this upset when your mother is her most..." he trailed off and shrugged, either unwilling or unable to finish the sentence.

"How do you know?" she asked. She didn't think she had ever told him anything about her mother or their strife-filled relationship.

He tilted his head at her. "Bronwyn, come on. I've known you forever. Do you think I was impervious to what went on in your house, to the way your mother treated you? She says horrible things that hurt and upset you, and it bothers me. A lot."

"It does?"

"Of course it does," he said. He was looking at her like she was crazy. Her brain felt foggy. "You're my baby," he added. His other hand eased to her neck, using it to pull her closer, and then he kissed her.

Bronwyn started to respond to him and then almost immediately pulled away. They were in Julian's guest bedroom, and it felt odd.

"I have news that might make you feel better," Carlo said, clasping her hand.

"What's that?" she asked, ridiculously glad for any distraction.

He picked her hand up and held it to his chest. "I made partner," he whispered.

Bronwyn froze, not sure she'd heard him correctly. "What? Are you serious?"

He nodded.

She tackled him, knocking him backwards onto the bed. "That's amazing and incredible. It's momentous."

"That's a lot of adjectives," he said, laughing as he caught her and pulled her onto his chest.

"Carlo, I am so thrilled for you, and so proud of you." She pressed her lips to his, a kiss of congratulations and excitement.

"Thank you," he said when the kiss was over. "I wanted you to be the first to know. I haven't even told my mom yet."

She cradled his face in her hands and kissed him again, lightly. "That's just...I am so incredibly happy for you, and so incredibly proud. This is it, you've accomplished your five year plan."

"Not all of it," he said, stroking his finger on her cheek.

Bronwyn swallowed hard, feeling suddenly flushed and overheated.

"I was going to ask you to go out to celebrate, but we can postpone if you're not feeling up to it."

"No, I want to," she said sincerely. Not only did she want to celebrate Carlo's amazing news, she selfishly wanted to run from her thoughts and feelings for as long as possible. "Let's go home and I'll freshen up." She slid off the bed and left the room, Carlo in her wake.

Julian sat in the living room, knitting. "Bronwyn and I are going out. Would you like to join us?" Carlo offered. Bronwyn was surprised by the gesture, but she didn't know why she should have been. Carlo was sweet and thoughtful and kind, and he and Julian were friends.

"Thanks, but you two kids go out and have fun while Grandpa stays home to knit." He looked up at them with a smile, his gaze shifting to Bronwyn. "Doing okay, kiddo?"

She nodded, not making eye contact. If she looked at him, really looked at him, she would break, and she didn't want to.

"All right. Have fun," he added.

"Thanks," Carlo said. He took Bronwyn's hand and led her to her house where she put on a fresh dress, brushed her teeth, washed her face, and re-did her makeup. It wasn't as good as a shower, but she didn't want to have to make Carlo wait longer than necessary.

They had a pleasant, fun evening together. Carlo was excited over his news, and Bronwyn was able to push everything away and focus on being happy for him. They both had work the next day, so it wasn't a late night. He walked her to the door and kissed her. She watched him drive away, waving, and then turned, crossed the hedge, and let herself in to Julian's house.

He was still on the couch, though now he had swapped out his knitting for a book. At the sight of Bronwyn, he set aside the book and opened his arms to her. She sat in his lap, resting her head on his chest.

"How was your night?" he asked.

"Good. Carlo made partner."

"That's momentous," he said. She laughed. It ended on a sob, and she finally let herself cry. Julian rubbed her back, and it was nice, but his silent, comforting presence was even better. Finally, when she had cried herself out, she sat quietly in his lap, staring at nothing.

"How do I go on after this?" she whispered.

"The same way we do everything else—one day at a time."

Yes. She could see it now, she would merely keep going on, and she would be fine. "How do you always know what I need to hear?"

"Those ESP classes are really paying off," he said, giving her a squeeze. He petted her head a while, almost absently, as if she were a cat. "Now that Carlo's made partner, I imagine he's going to want to put down roots."

"I imagine," she agreed. He had hinted at as much tonight, at their future.

"What will you say when he asks you to marry him, Bronwyn?"

"That's not a question I can answer in the hypothetical, Julian."

"Hmm," he said, his hand continuing to make absent passes over her head.

"What?" she said, rather snappishly. Did he think it was odd she didn't know? Would he tell her if she couldn't say yes in the hypothetical, she wasn't ready to say yes in reality?

"I was wondering which one I'll be, his best man or your mister of honor."

Bronwyn laughed and slung her arms around his neck, pressing her nose to his cheek. "Dibs on my mister," she said. She kissed his cheek, let him go, and went home to bed.

# CHAPTER 23

The following Sunday, Bronwyn sat in church sandwiched between her mother and Carlo. Her entire family was there—all the siblings, in-laws, and grandchildren. It had been her idea for everyone to make an appearance, so there was no way she could skip out, though she wasn't up to seeing anyone in her family, least of all her mother.

Carlo's arm around her shoulders felt reassuring and pleasant. "First time in a protestant church?" she whispered at the sudden remembrance he was Catholic.

He nodded.

"What do you think?" she asked.

"Easier on the knees," he whispered, and she smiled. At some point, if they stayed together, they would have to make a hard decision about religion. Did she see herself becoming Catholic? Did Carlo see himself becoming protestant? It was an age-old question, five hundred years, to be precise.

"What are you thinking?" he whispered.

"Medieval thoughts," she answered. He tilted his head at her in question, and she couldn't help but think Julian would have gotten her reference to the Reformation. "Nothing, never mind."

"Twenty years ago I think your mother never would have imagined we would arrive at this moment, me beside you in your church with my arm around you," he whispered.

"She might not have imagined it, but I did," Bronwyn whispered.

"Me too," he replied, giving her shoulders a squeeze.

The pleasant, peaceful moment was marred by the sight of her father reaching for her mother's hand, and her mother giving it with a smile. She looked the part of the perfect wife, mother, and grandmother. No one would ever guess what Bronwyn now knew, no one who wasn't privy to her mother's deep hypocrisy. There was a part of Bronwyn that wanted to take what she knew to the press and blurt. It would be satisfying to reveal her mother's lies, but only for a moment because it would hurt everyone else she knew and loved—her father, her siblings, her nieces and nephews, the people working on the campaign, Jeffrey's wife and children. A moment of vindication wasn't worth a lifetime of pain for everyone else, no matter how badly Bronwyn might want it.

She stuffed it down, deep down, and tried to pretend it didn't exist. If it had only been church, it might have been easier to do, but her mother had invited everyone back to their DC house for a lunch she cooked herself. Laurel was a talented cook, though she had lacked time in recent years to do it often. It was especially bittersweet today to taste food that reminded her of her childhood and a time when she was still innocent of the knowledge she now possessed. She watched as her mother buzzed around the room, hostessing with aplomb, being the perfect mother and grandmother, pausing to have meaningful contact with every member of the family.

When it was Bronwyn's turn, she beamed. "Well, if it isn't my favorite couple. You two were looking especially cozy today. Any particular reason?" Her eyes rested on Bronwyn's left hand, causing her to squirm uncomfortably.

"Carlo made partner, Mom. We've been pretty excited."

"As well you should be. That's marvelous news, Carlo. Congratulations," she said, pulling him into a tight, motherly hug. And then she hugged Bronwyn the same, and Bronwyn squeezed her eyes closed, gritting her teeth to keep herself from saying something she'd regret.

When her mother moved on, Carlo was watching her, his look probing and intent. "Bronwyn, what is wrong? You've been off the last few days, and I know something happened. Won't you please tell me?"

There was no safe place to talk inside. Bronwyn led him onto the porch, double checking the door to make sure they were alone. They sat on the swing.

"I found out something about my mom, and it's been a bit hard to deal with," she said.

He was quiet a few beats, absorbing. "Is it about Jeffrey?"

She turned to look at him, but he was staring at the far wall so she studied his perfect profile. "You knew?"

He nodded.

"Julian?" she guessed.

"My mom," he said.

Bronwyn closed her eyes and let out a breath. Of course Louisa knew. She knew everything about their family. "I don't know how to function around her now. The hypocrisy is revolting."

He clasped her hand and gave it a squeeze. "That's true, but you are the same."

"Am I? If the things that are foundational to my life aren't real, who am I?" she asked.

He gave her hand another squeeze. They sat in comfortable silence a while longer, swinging.

"Can I ask you a question?" he asked at last.

"Yes."

"This is what you were upset about the other night?"

"Yes."

"And Julian knew, it's why you were at his house?"

"Yes."

"Why didn't you tell me then?" he asked.

"I didn't want to mar your happy news," she said.

"Is that the only reason?" he pressed.

"What other reason would there be?" she countered.

He studied her. "Sometimes it seems you're more comfortable confiding in Julian than you are me."

"Julian and I are friends. It's different," she said.

"Should it be, though?" he asked.

"I'm sorry," she said, feeling exhausted.

"I'm not trying to wring an apology out of you here, that's not what this is about," he said, sounding uncharacteristically frustrated. Or maybe it was characteristic and she didn't know. If her mother's façade was so good, how did she know Carlo's wasn't? What if he had a raging temper and she had simply never seen it? He was always so perfect, so gentle, so kind, so caring and easygoing, but how could one person be so good? Was he too good? Was he fake? But, no, Julian trusted him, and Julian's intuition about people was spot on.

"What is this about?" she asked, somewhat belatedly because she had been staring at him in suspicious silence while she thought.

"Would you agree we're on a path here, Bronwyn?"

Her heart thundered, lodging in her throat and cutting off speech. She nodded.

"Then I guess I need to know from you that, even if I don't rank first in your heart now, I will someday," he said.

"Carlo," she breathed, letting go his hand to ease her arms around his neck. "I am genuinely sorry I made you feel second place to Julian. The way I view you two, it's different, very, very different." She kissed him and he responded. Bronwyn tried hard not to be relieved he hadn't asked her to define exactly which way she felt about each of them. At the moment, she wasn't sure she had an answer. But she was sure, in time, everything would sort itself out.

⚷

*L*ater, she let herself in to Julian's house exhausted. The day had been an emotionally wrenching train wreck, first with her family and then with Carlo. After their conversation on the porch, she had been careful to keep things upbeat, to pay close and special attention to him so he wouldn't feel slighted.

"How was lunch with the Porters?" Julian asked.

"Excellent, like being a POW with better food. We should do that every day, or at least until I have to be institutionalized for depression and anxiety," she said.

"So until tomorrow then," he guessed, setting his book aside.

Bronwyn blew out a breath. "Who are you, Julian?"

"I am Julian Baxter, son of Congresswoman Evelyn Baxter, drug addicted, alcoholic child of privilege who has failed everything and everyone in every way. I'm trying my best to take life one day at a time and love the people in it. If I do that well, I'll consider my life a raging success." He took her hand. "And who are you, Bronwyn?"

"I'm Bronwyn Porter, a total screw-up with absolutely zero career ambition. I'm too soft and way too trusting and my heart aches all the time with disappointment in humanity. Recently I started on a journey to figure out who I am, and so far I like me better than I ever imagined. And if I love people half as well as you do, I'll consider *my* life a raging success."

"Well, there you go. It looks like we've found the antidote to hypocrisy."

"Should we call a press conference, alert the world?" she asked.

"No, I'm planning to write a tell all."

"You are?"

He nodded. "It will be all about how I became best friends with my enemy."

"Sounds like a cliché," she said.

"No, I'm going to give it a twist ending." He brought her palm to his mouth and kissed it.

"What's that?" she asked, her heart thundering in her ears.

"Turns out she was a dude the whole time, then we start a basketball team together and win the Olympics. When I sell the movie rights, I'll give you a percentage."

She chortled. "Don't you think that's a bit far fetched?"

"It's more believable than the truth—that the person I needed most in the world was right next door the whole time." He brought her other palm to his mouth and kissed it. The hum was there again, only this time it was more like popcorn, jumping and snapping between them.

"Julian," she breathed, and then her phone buzzed with a text that made them both freeze. By now he knew when it was Laurel. He reached for his book and sat back.

"Better take it before she sends out the hounds," he said.

"Uh-oh," Bronwyn said.

"What?" he asked.

She held the phone aloft for him to read. *My office, first thing tomorrow.* "What do you suppose that's about?"

They made eye contact. "She knows," Julian said.

"She knows," Bronwyn agreed.

"Are you going to counter with what you know about her?" Julian asked.

The temptation was there, but at last she shook her head. "I don't play like that. I'll take it on the chin and move on."

"She's going to demand we never see each other again."

Bronwyn snorted. "I'd like to see her try."

"You will," Julian said.

# CHAPTER 24

Bronwyn thought she wouldn't be able to sleep because the anticipation of confronting her mother might weigh her down. But as soon as she left Julian's and got into bed, she was out and slept soundly until morning.

She arrived early, but her mother was already there and waiting on her. She closed the door to her office, pulled out a manila folder, and slapped it on the table between them.

"Explain these," Laurel said.

Bronwyn opened the folder and saw pictures of her and Julian staring back at her. They had been taken on various days in various situations, but in each one they were laughing together. She smiled.

"Well?" Laurel prompted.

Bronwyn looked up. "Explain why a photographer followed me, took pictures, and sent them to you."

Laurel paused. She had clearly not expected anything but for Bronwyn to fall all over herself in fear and sorrow. "I don't control every photographer in the nation, Bronwyn. I'm not William Randolph Hearst. They see something interesting, they send it my way for comment or approval. I happened to intercept these before they went to press. Can you imagine if I didn't?"

"We're friends," Bronwyn said.

"Does Carlo know?"

"Julian's the one who brought Carlo back into my life."

That gave Laurel another pause, and she blinked her way through it, processing. "Look, I can see the appeal of rebelling against me. We haven't always had the easiest time of things. But this, this is hitting below the belt, even for you, Bronwyn. What were you thinking becoming friends with this boy? I mean, really? Do you have any idea what this could do to my campaign?"

"Help it?" Bronwyn guessed.

"Not cute."

"I'm not trying to be, Mom. What is so bad about me being friends with Julian?"

"He's the enemy," Laurel hissed.

"He's not my enemy. He's my best friend."

Laurel reared back as if she'd been slapped. She was shaking her head furiously. "No, absolutely not, I forbid it. End it."

"No."

Laurel's mouth drew into a hard line. "End it or your fired."

"Fine, I'll clear out my desk," Bronwyn said. She stood, walked to her desk, and opened the drawers, searching for anything that was actually hers. There was nothing, save her stainless steel water flask. She should be upset, but really she was relieved. It was over. She had tried to assimilate into her mother's life, and she had failed. It was always a long shot. At least now she was free to move on and figure out what to do with the next phase of her life. Julian's words about teaching preschool kept ringing in her ears. She wouldn't make a lot doing that, but she could get roommates and live on the cheap in the city somewhere.

Out of the corner of her eye, she saw Jeffrey scurry into Laurel's office. Bronwyn turned away, not wanting to think what they might be doing behind closed doors. She picked up her purse and water bottle. She was about to say goodbye to the team when Jeffrey hurried out of the office, clamped his hand on her bicep, and dragged her back to her mother.

Once inside the office, he let her go and leaned against Laurel's desk. "Bronwyn, your mother has something to say to you," he said. He gave Laurel a prompting look. It was so reminiscent of the way Bronwyn's father handled her mother when they disagreed that Bronwyn swallowed hard and looked away. How deep did their relationship go? Was it merely physical, or did they love each other?

"Bronwyn, you can imagine my shock at seeing those pictures, at knowing you'd been fraternizing with the enemy," Laurel said, her temper beginning to rise again. Jeffrey cleared his throat, and she took a breath. "Anyway, I acted rashly, and I apologize. We'd like you to stay on. Of course we would prefer you not flaunt your friendship with that…that boy."

"I have never flaunted my friendship with Julian. We merely live our lives the best way we can, and we're always discreet when we go out. We'll continue to be discreet." *You know a thing or two about discretion, don't you, Mom?* It was on the tip of her tongue to say the words, and it took everything in her power not to.

"Good, then I think we're done here," Jeffrey said, probably sensing correctly he could only keep a cap on the tension between the two women for so long before it bubbled over again. "You're doing a good job, Bronwyn, and we appreciate it."

"Thank you, Jeffrey." It was hard not to put emphasis on *Jeffrey.* Shouldn't it have been her mother who said those words to her? "I'm keeping these." She reached for the folder on the desk and stuffed it into her purse.

When she left her mother's office a second time, she received a text from Julian.

*Dying here.*

*It's over,* she replied.

*Us or your life? Or your mom's life? You're not in jail are you, because I swore I would never go back.*

*She fired me then un-fired me,* Bronwyn told him. *Thanks to Jeffrey.*

*Ew.*

*I know, right? Celebration dinner tonight, you, me, and Carlo?* she said.

*Fantastic. I'm going to spend the rest of the day getting pretty for you.*

*Does that mean you're going to shower?* she asked.

*Don't be needy, baby. Doesn't suit. XO. J.*

The next morning when Julian woke, he found a framed picture on his bedside. It was a picture of him and Bronwyn, both laughing, their eyes sparkling as they looked at each other. He smiled and spied the note she'd left for him.

*This was my favorite, so very us. PS. Adore you more. PPS. If we have paparazzi, does it mean we've arrived? PPPS. You're a heavy sleeper, too. PPPPS. And cute. PPPPPS. It's annoying after the first PS, so stop it.*

He kissed his finger, touched it to picture Bronwyn's face, and set it back on his nightstand.

# CHAPTER 25

"Can I ask a favor?" Bronwyn asked Julian a few days after the meeting with her mother.

"Is it a kidney? Because you can have it, but you should know the drug and alcohol years did a lot of damage. Reasonably, it probably only has a few good years left, along with my liver and pancreas. Pretty much all my internal organs sustained damage, except my spine. Would you like it?"

"No, Carlo and I…"

"Found out you can't have children and need me to be the father. The answer is yes, but only if we go about it the old fashioned way. Our baby will not be made in a test tube."

She pinched his lips. "Maybe wait until I get the words out before adding your own. Carlo and I would like to cook supper for Louisa." She let go his lips. He squinted.

"What does that have to do with me?"

"We'd like you to be there," she said.

"I know we're all good friends and one big happy family, but isn't that a little weird?" he said.

"No, hear me out. It's always nerve wracking to meet the mother of the man you're dating."

"But you've known Louisa most of your life," he said.

"How is that hearing me out? Yes, I've known Louisa most of my life, but in the capacity as my maid. And now she's the mother of the guy I'm dating."

He gave her a look. "The word is boyfriend. What's so hard about it?"

"Being the first to say it," she said. "The point is I can't exactly have her over to my house and cook dinner, knowing she'll likely be the one to clean it up the next day. So I thought we could do it here and you could join and then it will be casual and friendly, less pressure."

He grinned at her.

"What?" she snapped.

"You're scared of Louisa," he said.

"No, I love Louisa. I'm scared of the mother of the man I'm dating. It's different."

He thought about it a minute. "That would be okay, as long as I can bring someone."

She tipped her head at him. "Who do you want to bring?"

"A friend."

"A girl friend?"

"I don't want to be the first to say the words," he said.

"You met someone?" she asked.

"No, I was making fun of you and your reluctance to call a spade a spade. I already know the person I'm going to bring, I've known her a long time."

"Who is it?"

"Maybe I don't want to tell you," he said.

"Why not?"

"Because she's special, and I don't want to ruin it."

Bronwyn's stomach pitched, at the thought of a stranger intruding in their perfectly formed group, she was certain. "Please tell me about her so I'm not blindsided."

"Why would it matter if my friend is blindsided?" he asked, and now he was the one to tip his head, studying her.

"I'm going to have a lot going on that night, lots of nerves and pressure. I don't want the stress of meeting a stranger I know nothing about on top of it," she said.

He took a breath and let it out. "Fine. Her name is Sabrina. She was my sober coach."

"Your sober coach?"

"Yes. We spent a ton of time together back when I was first getting sober. As you can imagine, I was kind of a mess and not in the right frame of mind to form relationships. But I've been thinking about her a ton. I really miss her, and I'd like to reconnect."

"Oh."

"What? You think it's weird to spend the evening with my sober coach?" he pressed.

"No, not at all."

"Then what's the deal? You look like you swallowed a live squid."

"I…I just…I didn't know you were looking for someone."

"I wasn't looking for someone. I told you, I've known her a long time, and I've been thinking about her a lot lately." He let out a breath. "To tell you the truth, I miss her. A lot. She's kind of amazing. You'll see when you meet her."

"Is she, you know, going to think it's weird we're friends?"

"No, she's not political at all. I seriously doubt she has any idea who you are."

"I didn't mean that. I meant will she think it's weird you and I are close?" she asked.

"Oh, I guess I didn't think about that. But it's probably fine, right? Carlo doesn't think it's weird, doesn't feel threatened by me, does he?" he asked.

"I don't think so, but you and Carlo are friends," she said.

"I'm sure you and Sabrina will be friends eventually. I want all the important people in my life to be friends," he said.

Bronwyn nodded absently. "Is she pretty?"

"She's gorgeous," he said.

"Is she your type?"

"I don't have a type. What's with all the questions, Bronwyn? Do you not want her to come? Because I haven't said anything to her yet, but if it bothers you, I won't do it."

"Of course it doesn't bother me. Why would it bother me? Does it bother you when Carlo and I are together?"

"Why would it bother me?" he countered.

"Great. Neither of us is bothered. Bring your pretty, perfect friend."

"Great," he said, beaming at her in a way that made her want to punch him more than a little.

To her further annoyance, Carlo was equally delighted over the prospect. "It doesn't bother you?" Bronwyn asked him.

"Why should it? I'm sure he's been lonely with us dating. When we do get together, he must feel like a third wheel," Carlo said. He was in the midst of checking his work messages on his phone.

"Because I'm meeting your mother."

He laughed. "Bronwyn, you've known my mother almost as long as I have."

"But it's different. I was hoping for support, moral support, and instead he's bringing some little dish to moon over."

"Little dish to moon over? Are you in a black and white movie from the forties?" Carlo asked.

"We don't know anything about this woman, and now she's suddenly a huge part of his life?" Bronwyn said.

"*Querida*, I don't think everyone has to date someone they've known for a minimum of two decades," he said.

"What's the Spanish word for patronizing?" she asked.

He finally glanced up from his phone. "Are we fighting?"

"Of course not," she huffed, crossing her arms over her chest.

"Could we? Because I would love to make up." He set aside his phone and reached for her, pressing his lips to her neck.

"How can you be irresistible when I'm being a pill?" she asked.

"Why exactly are you being a pill, your word, not mine?" He eased back so he could see her face while keeping her in his arms.

"I have no idea, but I promise to stop." She stood on her toes and pressed a kiss to his lips, and the subject was dropped, for Carlo, at least. Bronwyn was still puzzled by her behavior. She was the fourth in a family of six, not exactly immune to being one in a crowd. She had never needed to be one of those women who had to be the center of attention, and certainly not male attention. Why now was she having what amounted to a hissy fit at the thought of Julian bringing a date?

She wouldn't be, she determined. She wouldn't mention it to Julian or Carlo again. But in her mind, she couldn't seem to let it go. Who was Sabrina the Magnificent? How serious was Julian about her?

On the night of the dinner, both men left Bronwyn at Julian's house. She worked to finish dinner while Carlo went to retrieve Louisa and Julian went for his date. When the door opened, she froze and braced herself, relaxing when it was Carlo and Louisa. "Hi," she greeted them, hurrying forward to take Louisa's coat and give her a hug.

"What can I do, *querida*?" Carlo offered, snagging a grape from the basket on the counter.

"Nothing. I think I'm well in hand here, thank you."

"Carlo is a good cook," Louisa added helpfully. "I made sure all my children know how to cook and clean and do their own laundry."

"You did perfectly, Louisa. Carlo is an a amazing b..." she caught herself before she could call him her boyfriend. Always before Bronwyn had pushed men away by getting too serious, too soon, by digging her claws in and clinging. Now that she had a better under-standing of herself and the world in general, she vowed not to do it again. Therefore she absolutely refused to be the first one to define their relationship, no matter how much Julian teased her about it. "Carlo is an amazing person."

"Are you afraid to use gender pronouns in front of my mother?" he teased.

"Carlo is an amazing man," Bronwyn amended, leaning forward to kiss his cheek. Louisa, meanwhile, beamed an approving look between them.

The happy moment ended when the door opened and Julian arrived with his date. "Everyone, this is Sabrina." He moved aside to reveal a heavyset black woman who was easily sixty years old. She beamed at them and gave a friendly hello. Bronwyn returned her hello. She tried to avoid Julian's eyes but couldn't, and when she looked at him he was giving her a satisfied, knowing smile. In response, she turned her back on him and finished her meal prep.

Sabrina was as delightful as Julian had said she would be, pleasant, friendly, funny, and outgoing. She was happily married, had four children, and had been a sober coach for ten years. Bronwyn could definitely see why. She was the type of person who would be wonderful to have around when life was glum and the chips were down.

"Bronwyn, for a skinny white girl, you can cook," she said about halfway through the evening.

"Told you you were skinny," Julian added, but Bronwyn ignored him, as she had been doing the entire evening.

"Too skinny," Louisa piped up. "You need to put some meat back on, Niña."

"You guys are confusing me. I'm not sure if I'm actually thin or if I've been hanging around with the wrong culture my entire life," Bronwyn said.

"Maybe it's a combination," Carlo said, pinching her waist affectionately.

"How do you explain me?" Julian asked.

"I don't," Bronwyn said before quickly directing a comment to someone else.

When the meal was finished, Bronwyn excused herself to go to the bathroom. She put it off until she couldn't any longer, and for good reason. As soon as she left the bathroom, Julian met her in the hallway.

"Why are you mad at me?" he asked, hustling her back into the bathroom and closing the door behind them.

"You can't corner me in the bathroom and close the door," she said, reaching for it.

He dodged in front of her, blocking her exit. "I'm the king of the castle, baby. I can do whatever I want." As if to prove it, he picked her up and set her on the counter in front of him. "Now, why are you being so snippy with me?"

"You know why," she said.

"Tell me in your own words," he prompted.

"You knew I thought you were bringing a real date tonight."

"Sabrina's a real date. I picked her up, I provided dinner. If all goes well, I might try to kiss her good night, as long as her husband isn't looking out the window. He's huge, could literally rip my face off and feed it to their dog."

"Julian, why did you trick me?" she asked.

"I didn't trick you. I didn't say one single thing that wasn't true. I really like Sabrina. I have really missed Sabrina. Sabrina is lovely and gorgeous. Tell me which part of that isn't true."

"The intent. You told me all that stuff about her to make me jealous, to make me crazy."

"Did it work?"

She looked away from him, down and to the side. "Yes."

"To answer your question, the reason I did it was because teasing you makes my life worth living, because the angry little flush of your cheeks makes my heart go pitty pat. I guess now the question you need to ask yourself, Bronwyn," he touched his finger under her chin and tipped her face toward his, "is why it worked."

His finger was still under her chin, their faces were a half inch apart, so close she could feel the warmth of his breath on her mouth. Her lips parted, and so did his. Her hand reached out, but before either of them knew where it might land, Carlo called her name.

"Bronwyn, *querida*, are you coming with me to take my mother home?"

"Yes," she whispered, her eyes still locked with Julian's.

"He can't hear you," Julian whispered. "Or were you not talking to him?"

She peeled her eyes away from his and faced the door. "Yes, I'm coming," she called, louder this time.

Julian put out a hand. She took it and jumped down off the counter. He held the door for her, and she preceded him through.

It was their custom to check in with each other before bed, to have a recap of their days and say goodnight. But when Bronwyn returned from taking Louisa home, she didn't go to Julian's. Instead she went straight to bed. She was exhausted, but instead of sleep, she stared hard at the ceiling, trying not to think of anything at all.

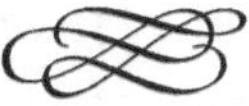

# CHAPTER 26

The next day, Bronwyn intended to avoid Julian. But he showed up bright and early on her doorstep with a box of scones from the local bakery.

"You can't avoid me," he said, tossing the box onto the table.

"It's six in the morning," she said, still groggy from her lousy night of sleep. "And I'm getting ready for work."

"You don't leave for another forty minutes, and I know you. You were intending to avoid me."

She took a breath and let it out slowly, looking away from him. "Julian..."

"Bronwyn, don't. Let's face some cold, hard facts. Fact: you are a woman."

She sat up in surprise. "I am? This explains so much about all those locker room mixups and fiascos."

"I am a man." She opened her mouth to say something else, but he clamped his fingers on her lips. "Second fact: we're both deliriously attractive. Things are going to happen sometimes."

She pushed his hand off her lips. "Things can't happen sometimes or any time. I'm with Carlo."

"I know, and I love Carlo. He's one of my best friends. Hence, the scones." He tapped the box on the table.

"What do scones have to do with Carlo?" she asked, reaching for one.

"Scones say I'm sorry we're attracted to each other sometimes and might accidentally trod on your relationship with your boyfriend who hasn't yet called himself your boyfriend."

"Chatty scones," she commented taking a bite.

He poured them each a mug of coffee and set hers before her, giving her a sideways hug around the shoulders as he did so. "It's nature, baby. We're two pretty people in the prime of our lives. We find each other attractive. So what, big deal. Lots of attractive people out there. All we have to do is be careful not to let it be a problem."

"This would all be more believable from you if you weren't staring down the front of my nightgown as you're saying it."

"Who answers the door in a nightie?" he accused.

"I didn't answer the door—you broke in, you sneaky unreformed thief."

"I don't think someone who breaks in to deliver scones can be considered a thief," he said. "And why are you wearing such sexy lingerie anyway?"

"This is a Harvard nightshirt I've had since I was fourteen years old. I found it in the back of my drawer."

"Exactly, you know I think smart girls are hot, and yet you torment me. Why, Bronwyn, why do you do me this way? A man can only take so much," he said.

"You're going to need a lot more scones," she said, tossing a wadded up napkin at him.

"Let me add meat into the mix. Have dinner with me tonight," he said.

"Are you sure that's a good idea?" she asked. Lately they hadn't done such a good job of keeping the attraction between them to a simmer.

"Yes, it's like with the booze. Resisting you is one more temptation I need to work on, like building muscle memory."

"Are you trying to tell me you're addicted to me?" she teased.

"Yes," he answered, dead serious.

"What kind of needlework are you going to take up to replace me?"

He reached for her hand and brought it to his lips. "Honey, there's not enough yarn in the world for that."

Bronwyn stood and mussed his hair, keeping the moment light before it could go somewhere neither of them could undo. It wasn't up to him alone to keep them out of trouble. She needed to build her muscle memory, too.

Later, they met back up at her house. They were in the midst of deciding where to eat that night when Carlo walked into the kitchen. "Hey, did I know you were coming tonight?" Bronwyn asked.

"No, I thought I would stop in and see if you were available," Carlo replied.

"Julian and I were going to hang out, but we could all hang out together. It could be like old times, only not really because back then it was me spying on you two in secret. But this will be nice, too."

"That sounds good, *querida*, but as I was pulling in, your mother arrived behind me."

"Ding, dong, the witch is here," Julian said. "And that's my cue to go." He took a step away, but Bronwyn grabbed him back.

"Hang on, sassy pants. Stay."

"That nickname only works when I use it on you," he said. "Are you sure you're ready for this?"

"Ready? Are you joking? I lost bladder control a little bit. But that's kind of the thing; I'll never be ready. Might as well get it over with and face it head on, right?" She turned to Carlo who shrugged help-lessly. "Right?" this time she faced Julian.

"Right," he agreed. "Being brave, good."

Their bravado was ruined when Louisa skidded into the kitchen. "*Niña, tu madre* is here. Julian, *hide*."

"It's okay, Louisa. We're facing it head on."

"It's not okay. She will kill us all and eat our livers for breakfast," Louisa hissed.

Bronwyn laughed. "I really think it's going to be all right. You can hide in the other room until it's over, if you want. For safety."

Louisa squared her shoulders. "No. I will stay and work in the background. Perhaps if I am here, she will go softer on you."

Suddenly Bronwyn's memory flashed to all the times her mother had reamed her while Louisa hovered anxiously in the background. Had she been attempting to offer protection then, too? "Louisa, I love you so."

"*Y tu, Niña*," Louisa said as she picked up a sponge and scrubbed at an invisible spot on the counter. Everyone else faced the door.

"This is like waiting for the Death Star to land," Julian said.

"That's true. My mom bears a striking resemblance to Darth Vader in three inch heels."

"Why is everyone staring at the door?" Laurel spoke from behind them. They had apparently been facing the wrong door. They whirled to face her, and that was when she caught sight of Julian. "What's he doing here?"

"I invited him," Bronwyn said.

"Out, get out."

"No." It was the first time Bronwyn had ever said the word to her mother with so much force.

"No?" Laurel repeated as if she didn't understand it.

"I invited him. He's my friend. He stays."

"It's my house. You're my employee. He goes."

"I'm also your daughter. I know that counts for nothing in your mind, but you'd think common courtesy and manners would compel you to allow him to stay."

Laurel shook that off like a dog shaking water droplets. Unable to fathom Bronwyn's new demeanor, she turned her attention to Julian. "Out."

Bronwyn linked her arm with his. "No. He goes, I go."

"Fine, get out," Laurel said. Behind her Louisa hissed and pretended it was a cough.

"I think you're bluffing, Mom."

"Have you ever known me to bluff, Bronwyn?"

"Okay, let me revise. I don't think you're cognizant of what you're about to do here because I've brought you more votes than you had in your last campaign. If I go, I'm taking all those votes to his side." She pointed to Julian.

"Why are you doing this?" Laurel asked. "Is this how you treat your mother?"

"This is how I treat my friend, the way he deserves. This is how I show him the kind of loyalty he's shown me."

Laurel pinched the end of her nose. "Bronwyn, why do you always, always have to make everything so difficult?"

"It's called existing, Mom, and it's all I've ever tried to do. And somehow I did, despite how many times you tried to crush me, I kept springing back up. I'd say that kind of resilience means something."

"Hear, hear," Julian agreed.

"You stay out of this," Laurel hissed.

"He's in this," Bronwyn said. "He's so deep in this he can't even see the surface anymore."

"Why do you think that is, Bronwyn? You think his interest in you is altruistic? You think he's selfless?" She shook her head. "He's a spy, working for his mom's campaign, working against me. And if you're with him, then you're against me."

Bronwyn tried to think how best to counter her mother's attack, but instead she sidestepped it completely. "I know." Julian sucked in a little breath, shocked she had gone to the one place she didn't want to go.

"You know he's a spy?" Laurel said.

"No, Mom, I know. I know about you."

"What do you know about me?"

"I know you're having an affair with Jeffrey Clark. I know it's probably not the first affair you've had. And I begin to wonder how far back they go. Am I Dad's child? Because that would explain why you hate me so."

Quick as an adder, Laurel reared back her hand and slapped

Bronwyn hard across the cheek, so hard she saw stars and her teeth felt like they rattled. The motion swung her head to the side, to Carlo who stood frozen, his mouth open in shock. To her right, Julian lunged for Laurel. Before he could reach her, Louisa inserted herself between them.

"Help me," she hissed to her son. Carlo stepped forward to secure Julian.

"Easy, stop it, stop it," Louisa soothed.

"Not worth going back," Carlo said. Bronwyn realized he was talking about jail, and she snapped back into focus.

"Stop, please, please don't," she said, going forward to grasp his arm.

He stopped fighting them and went slack. She could both see and feel him struggling to get himself back under control. Everyone seemed unable to think what to do next. Eventually Julian spoke. "I'm okay, you can let me go." Everyone but Bronwyn let him go. He slid his arm around her and inspected her face.

"Are you badly hurt?" he asked, inspecting her face.

She couldn't make eye contact. If she did, she would lose it completely. *I'm a ping pong paddle. Deflect, bounce back, don't absorb it.* "I'm fine." He touched her cheek, the tender caress of his fingers sharp contrast to her mother's violent smack. When he was satisfied she was all right, he turned to Laurel. He raised a shaking finger and pointed it at her face.

"If you ever touch her again, I will destroy you."

She blew out a puff of air that was supposed to pass for a laugh, but Bronwyn could see the hint of fear in her eyes.

"You think I'm joking? I've watched this house for twenty years. I know all your secrets, all of them. If you lay a hand on her, if you speak to her the way you've always spoken to her, if you so much as look at her cross eyed, I will take those secrets to the long list of people in this town who owe me a favor. There are a lot of them, and it will end you. Do you understand me, Laurel, are we clear? I will end you." He said the last four words slowly and emphatically, his finger jutting in her face. Not waiting for an answer, he turned and left the house.

Laurel looked at the people in the room she could still control, the housekeeper and her child. "Louisa, Carlo, I need a moment alone with my daughter."

To Laurel's further annoyance, they looked at Bronwyn. She nodded, and they left the kitchen.

"I don't think I have to tell you how uncomfortable I am you chose to air our family's dirty laundry in front of a stranger and the help."

Bronwyn let out a sad little laugh. "A stranger and the help? Mom, those three people are more family to me than you've ever been."

"I don't understand where this is coming from. All I've ever done your entire life is try to help you. Why are you so ungrateful?"

"We're not even going to talk about the affair?"

"There is no affair. I'm not sure what your little Baxter friend told you, but it's a lie."

"You think Julian told me you were having an affair? No, Mom, my eyes and ears told me that. Julian stood in the pantry with me, holding his hands over my ears to try and protect them from hearing what was going on. I wish it had worked."

Laurel looked away. "Your father and I have been having some issues. They don't concern you."

"Fine," Bronwyn said. She didn't actually want to talk about her mother's affair. It was enough her mother knew Bronwyn was onto her. Laurel shifted from foot to foot. At first Bronwyn thought maybe it was guilt or remorse, but that notion was soon dispelled.

"Do you think he'll tell his mother's camp this information?"

"Is that really your main concern right now? That Julian will leak the news of your affair?"

"Yes, what else is there?" Laurel said.

Bronwyn sighed, feeling suddenly a thousand years old. "No, Mother. Julian would never hurt me that way."

"What does it have to do with you?" Laurel asked.

"Nothing." She turned to go.

"Bronwyn," her mother said.

Bronwyn froze and turned back.

"Your father is your father. There's no ambiguity on that."

"Thank you. I guess I'll have to keep searching for some other reason you hate me so much." Wearily, she turned and made her way from the room.

# CHAPTER 27

Julian had a hard time falling asleep. He went back to his house alone, shaken over the deep rage he had felt, over the urge to physically assault Laurel Portman. He had never liked the woman, never enjoyed her persistent attacks on his mother. But he had never felt the sort of vitriolic violence toward her he experienced when her hand connected with Bronwyn's face.

Bronwyn hadn't followed him home, and he was glad. He needed time to cool off, to work through the anger. He watched Bronwyn and Carlo get in his car, apparently for a night on the town after the disastrous meeting with her mother. He wasn't surprised or upset she didn't seek him out. He knew her well enough by now to understand she would need time to work through the painful event before they spoke about it, the same as he did.

Eventually he drifted off, only to wake an unknown time later to Bronwyn standing beside his bed. "I can't sleep," she whispered. "My mom's staying the night, and the house feels so…"

He moved aside the covers. She lay down beside him and curled into a ball, her fists at his chest. "Do you want to talk?" he asked.

"No."

"Do you want me to hold you?"

"More than anything."

He slid his arms around her, and they shifted, adjusting their positions until they were both comfortable. It happened faster and easier than he would have thought, as if they'd been sleeping side by side forever.

"You can cry, if you want to," he offered.

"Ping pong paddles don't cry," she reminded him.

"Their best friends do," he said.

She tilted her head to see him. "You cried for me?"

He nodded. "It hurt me to see you hurt that way. I'm an empath."

"That's a liberal mumbo jumbo word," she informed him, giving his side a light poke.

"What's the stuffy conservative way to describe me?" he asked, poking her in return.

"Perfection." They lay in silence a few minutes before she spoke again. "You want to know a secret, Julian?"

"Desperately."

He felt her smile against his chest, and he smiled in response. "The older I get, the more aligned I become with your way of thinking. We do have a responsibility to use our privilege for good, to affect social positive change, to take care of each other."

"You want to know my secret, Bronwyn? The same is true for me in reverse. Those things you said about having a family, about marriage and children, they resonated with me. It feels like all society's ills can be traced to the breakup of the family."

"It seems we've found common ground between our opposing sides. Should we tell someone?" she asked.

"Let's keep it to ourselves until the world is ready to hear it," he said.

"When will that be, do you think?"

"Two apocalypses from now," he said and she laughed.

"Are you going to tell Carlo we're having a sleepover?" he asked.

"Does Carlo know for certain you're straight?" she asked.

"Yes."

"Then no," she said. "I don't want him to get the wrong idea about us."

"The wrong idea, yes. As I was saying, strong, healthy relationships make the world go round," he said. His fingers sifted gently through her hair, making her sleepy.

"Julian," she said drowsily.

"Hmm," he said, equally as drowsy.

"This is nice."

"Bronwyn."

"Hmm."

"Yes it is."

A few minutes later, they were both asleep.

When Bronwyn woke the next morning, Julian was staring at her. "It's especially pleasant to wake to a beautiful woman beside me," he noted.

"When did I graduate from pretty to beautiful?" she asked.

"Hmm, let me ponder. About twenty seven years ago." She smiled. He reached for her hand, giving it a squeeze. "How are you?"

"I'm fine, truly," she said. "It was…"

He put a finger to her lips. "If you say it was no big deal, I'm kidnapping you and taking you to emergency therapy in Canada."

"Why Canada?"

"Socialized medicine. Therapy doesn't come cheap."

"Not as much of it as I'm going to need. But I was going to say it was nothing less than what I expected."

"Bronwyn, my sweet baby girl." He leaned forward and pressed his lips to hers. She could tell he meant it as a spontaneous, comforting gesture, but her lips clung to his, ruining the moment. Or perhaps not ruining it because he froze an inch from her face, staring.

"Um, do you think we…" she began.

He touched his fingers to her lips again and shook his head. "I think the portion of the morning for rational conversation is over.

Can I interest you in a rash, passionate gesture we may both soon regret?"

She nodded and closed her eyes, but nothing happened. She opened her eyes again and saw his face lingering near hers, a hairsbreadth away but not touching. "What are you doing?" she whispered.

"I'm letting the tension build," he said.

"Does that work?" she asked.

"One can only hope."

She snickered.

"I'm about to kiss you, woman. Don't make fun of my grammar," he chided.

"One will try," she promised. She closed her eyes and touched her palm to his cheek. He leaned forward and the door flew open.

"Julian, we're ho…."

His mother stood in the doorway, blinking furiously at them, trying to assimilate the scene before her. Bronwyn sat up. She was fully dressed, but she felt vulnerable and exposed as his mother's eyes roamed over her. Julian sat up beside her.

"Mom, this is Bronwyn Porter. Not sure you two have ever formally met."

The older woman continued to blink rapidly, her mouth agape. Finally she closed her mouth, swallowed convulsively, and spoke. "Welcome, Bronwyn. It's nice to meet you," her voice was raspy, but she got the words out and even managed to sound sincere.

Bronwyn slid out of the bed, went forward, and wrapped her in a tight hug. "Thank you," she whispered.

"For what?" Mrs. Baxter asked, patting Bronwyn's arm absently.

"For Julian." She turned to face him. Together, the two women stared at him. "You've had a lot of amazing accomplishments, Congresswoman Baxter, but Julian is by far your best."

"I think I might actually be blushing," Julian said.

"I think you might be," his mother agreed. "Not sure I've ever seen that happen before." She was still too startled to smile, but there was a hint of amusement in her tone. "And I'm inclined to agree with you, Bronwyn."

"Good luck on your campaign," Bronwyn said, turning to face her. "I realize you don't know me well enough to understand I'm not saying that sarcastically, but I'm not. You've run a tight campaign, and I wish you all the best, truly." She squeezed her hand and took a step toward the door.

"Thank you," Mrs. Baxter said.

"Wait a minute, where are you going? We were in the middle of something here. Why are you leaving?" Julian called.

Bronwyn paused by the door. "Because, Julian, *your mom*."

He rolled his eyes, laughing. "I told you never to use that as an answer again."

She tossed him a wave, her laughter echoing down the hall.

# CHAPTER 28

The following Saturday was the children's hospital fundraiser ball. It was a massive DC occasion, a bipartisan event. Everyone would be there, Laurel and Evelyn and their husbands, Bronwyn and Carlo, and even Julian.

"Anything for the kids," he had said when Bronwyn asked if he was going to go.

"And also for free cake, am I right?" she countered.

"You know it," he said, ending on a fist bump. But that had been weeks ago, before everything turned so tense and complicated between them. She hadn't seen or spoken to him since she left his room the morning of the almost kiss. Now, the evening of the ball, she let herself into his house and found him standing in his tux, staring at the computer. He turned to smile at her approach.

"Hey."

"Hey," she replied, relaxing a little. Things seemed to be back on even footing between them. "Could you finish zipping me? I can't reach."

"C'mere," he said, motioning her closer. She reached him and turned around. He zipped her, and there was an awkward pause when she thought he might be reaching for her. When he didn't, she turned back around.

"I don't suppose you know how to tie a bowtie," he said, motioning helplessly to his neck. "I was looking it up, but the directions don't make sense."

"I know how," she said. She reached for him, but he was tall. "A little help with the height, please."

He set her on the counter, and she focused on tying his tie. He was very close to her, his hands resting on the counter on either side of her hips. "Did I say you look amazing? I was thinking it in my head."

"Thank you. You look...you look so handsome, Julian." She finished with the tie and smoothed her hands down his arms, brushing at imaginary wrinkles.

"As handsome as Carlo?" he teased. Or was he teasing? Was it possible he thought he wasn't?

"Yes."

"I've never heard you say I was dreamy," he added.

"That's because you're not in my head." They stared at each other, the old, familiar tension as unbearable as ever.

"I'd say save me a dance tonight, but I don't think that's in the cards for us," he said.

"A dance would be nice, but you're right. I don't think we could pull it off, and I should go. Carlo will be here soon."

"Carlo's always here," Julian said, motioning between them. "Someone should have warned me."

"About what?" she asked, her heart thumping hard against her ribs.

"About how difficult it would be to be best friends with a pretty girl," he said. He plucked her off the counter, set her on the ground, and took a step away. "Have fun tonight."

"You, too," she said. She touched her palm to his cheek and let herself out.

Carlo was prompt, as usual, and dashingly handsome, also as usual. He greeted her with a kiss and then another. "Seeing you in that dress makes me think we are long overdue for a serious conversation," he said.

"Probably so," Bronwyn agreed.

He pulled back and studied her face. "Are you okay? The other night with your mother was…"

She didn't want to talk about the other night or her mother. Something was niggling in the back of her mind, something about Carlo, and she didn't want to think what it might be, didn't want to do anything but have fun and dance.

"I'm perfectly wonderful," Bronwyn said, slipping her arm through his.

The ball was crowded, and Bronwyn had never been more thankful for valet parking. Carlo tossed the guy his keys and held out his arm to her, escorting her inside.

The interior of the large hall was plush and decadent, but for five hundred dollars a head, it should be. Her mother had generously covered the cost for both her and Carlo, back before they had their confrontation, when things had been going well. She hadn't seen or talked to her mother since the night of their big blowup, and she wondered how it would be. She should have known it would be fine. Her mother was a consummate politician; no emotion leaked through when she greeted Bronwyn and Carlo, except possibly pleasure and a little bit of pride.

*She really, really, really likes me and Carlo together,* Bronwyn thought, but the thought didn't make her happy. If anything, it increased her discomfort and unease. Her mother had never been able to leave well enough alone. It was nearly miraculous she had done so little to meddle in her relationship with Carlo. Had she finally learned her lesson? Bronwyn pushed away her thoughts and scanned the room, waving and smiling at several familiar faces. Everyone was there, senators, congressmen, lobbyists. Even the president and his wife were slated to stop by later in the evening. Security was tight, and so was space. It was almost uncomfortably crowded. The only free space was on the dance floor where no one was yet dancing.

Bronwyn scanned the crowded room and finally saw Julian. He sat at a table alone, but his mother was nearby talking. He locked eyes with Bronwyn and smiled before turning his narrowed gaze to her mother. He shifted his eyes between them and raised his eyebrows at her. *Everything okay?*

She nodded. He raised two fingers to his eyes and pointed them at her mom, letting her know he'd be keeping an eye on things.

She directed her eyes between him and the drink table with the same questioning raise of eyebrows. He gave her the okay sign with his fingers. She pointed her fingers at her eyes and the drink table, letting him know she'd be watching. He tipped his seltzer glass to her, and she smiled before Carlo claimed her attention, pulling her away.

Carlo led her around, mingling for a long time. He would be good in politics, she now realized. He was pleasant and sharp and unobjectionable. Everyone liked him, everyone had a kind word for him, and he had one in reply. He was good at remembering names and faces, occasionally supplying them to Bronwyn when she forgot. Perhaps her mother's interest in him was about more than the Latinx vote; perhaps she had political plans for Bronwyn, plans that included Carlo by her side. It would be like her mother to want to pass on the throne to someone in the family, to create a political dynasty. The thought made Bronwyn queasy. She didn't want to go into politics. Did she?

Her mother made her way over. "Carlo, may I speak with my daughter a moment?" Her tone was breezy, but no less lacking in authority.

"I'll grab us a drink, shall I?" Carlo asked.

"Seltzer for me, please," Bronwyn said.

"I know, my baby," he said, giving her a hand a squeeze before walking away.

"He certainly is smitten," her mother commented.

When Bronwyn didn't reply, Laurel cleared her throat. "I need to apologize to you, Bronwyn. I shouldn't have hit you the other day."

"I wasn't exactly innocent, Mom. I said some fairly provoking things."

"They weren't altogether unjustified. The things that happen between a husband and wife are just that, between a husband and wife. They have nothing to do with you and me or you and your father."

"That's what Julian said," Bronwyn replied.

"Yes, well, anyway, I am sorry I hit you. I've never hit any of you in the face like that, and I feel very badly about it."

"Thank you."

There was another awkward pause before Laurel spoke again. "I also owe you an apology for the way I've treated you, like a child who doesn't know better. You've more than proved your capability. You've been a boon to my campaign, a godsend, really, and I'm thankful for you. I'm very proud of you."

They were the exact words Bronwyn had long waited to hear, and now that she was hearing them she felt numb. Maybe in time she would process them and they would fill all the places in her heart she needed them to, but for now they settled on top of her emotions like a layer of sunscreen.

"Thank you," Bronwyn remembered to add. Suddenly she was incredibly glad the election was only two weeks away. She would finish out her mother's campaign, and then she would move on with her life. She was done with politics, with trying to fit in a world that wasn't her own. For the first time in a long time, she began to feel excitement rather than fear over the prospect. She was twenty seven years old; she could do anything. Maybe at some point she would find some career ambition and finally figure out what she wanted to do.

Carlo returned, rescuing her from further conversation. They mingled for a while longer. Bronwyn put up a good front, but inside her mind wouldn't be still. It was all too much, and it was dogpiling on top of her at the worst possible moment—her mother's affair, the campaign, the slap, her mother's words, Carlo, Julian. She needed to breathe, to be alone, to gather her thoughts. But she couldn't. She was stuck, and the air was close, adding to her claustrophobia.

Bronwyn tensed as her mother approached them again, but she was still smiling. "No one is dancing. I would love to see you two on the floor." She put a hand on Carlo's shoulder and gave him a little shove forward.

"Shall we?" Carlo asked, holding out his hand to Bronwyn. She took it and allowed him to lead her onto the dance floor. A few cameras clicked, and she could picture tomorrow's headlines. The optics were good. Carlo was handsome and accomplished, an American dream come true. No wonder her mother couldn't stop smiling. This was a major coup for her campaign, a positive step toward securing a large portion of the Latinx vote.

"You look beautiful tonight, *querida*," Carlo whispered.

"Thank you," Bronwyn replied. She smiled up at him, albeit sadly.

"What is wrong?" he asked.

"Have you ever heard that proverb 'be careful what you wish for because you might get it'?" Bronwyn said.

"Yes, but I've never understood it. How could it be bad to get all the things you want?"

"I think maybe because by the time you get them, you've changed so much you don't need them anymore," she said.

"What? Bronwyn, what is the matter?"

"I have this horrible inability to turn off my brain," she said.

"You have a headache?" he asked, tilting his head at her in concern.

"No. I've been thinking too much."

"About me?" he said, his tone flirtatious.

"Yes."

His smile faltered. "Sweetheart, have I done something to upset you?"

"The other day, when my mother hit me, you stood perfectly still. You did nothing."

He winced, a bit self-deprecatingly, she thought. "It seemed unwise to tackle my girlfriend's mother."

He had never called her his girlfriend before. The girly part of her heart that had been waiting for the words did a little cartwheel at that, but she shoved it aside. "I might believe that if I didn't know you."

"What do you mean?" he asked.

"I watched you grow up, Carlo, and crushed on you all of that time. And the main reason was not because of your devastating good looks, though that's definitely an added bonus. The main reason was because of something I saw one day when you stood at your bus stop. I used to make a sport of spying on you. On this particular day someone was picking on someone smaller. You tackled him, punched him in the face, told him never to do it again. I thought it was the bravest, most spectacular thing I ever saw because you were someone who stood up for the underdog, an underdog like me."

"Bronwyn," he began, his tone sounding pained now.

"Why did you make partner so many years ahead of schedule?" she blurted.

He froze, hitching slightly in the dance, forcing her to stop before she stumbled over his feet. "The partners decided…" His tone was faltering, and she knew.

"The senior partner in your firm is named Clark, the same last name as Mom's campaign manager. She fixed it for you, offered them promises in exchange for the partnership."

He licked his lips. "She thought it would be best, since you and I were together, that I have a more prestigious position in the firm."

"Oh, Carlo. Do you not understand I wanted to be with you no matter what? I don't want the title. I don't want the prestige." She stopped dancing and took a step back out of his embrace.

"Bronwyn, I would have made partner eventually."

"That's what's so heartbreaking—I know you would. You're crazy smart and talented and amazing at your job. You're amazing all around, kind and deep and fun and funny." Tears flooded her eyes. She blinked them away.

"This has nothing to do with us," he said.

"It has everything to do with us," she countered. "My entire existence, my mother has been arranging my life, either through nagging or outright manipulation. She has ruined everything for me, everything. She has poisoned the well in every aspect of my life, every job, every relationship. There isn't one piece of my life she's left untouched." She paused, her lips turning up slightly. "No, I guess there's one piece."

"Please don't let this come between us. Things have been so good."

"I thought you were different. I thought you were outside my mother's reach, what we had was only between us. But I was wrong. How can I trust this is real when I know my mother bought you off?" she asked.

He flinched. "It's not like that. Do you think my interest in you is sudden? Do you think you're the only one who watched when we were kids? The only one with a crush? Julian and I used to talk about…" he broke off, swallowing convulsively. He took a breath and tried again. "I love you."

"Thank you," she whispered. "That's very kind and always nice to hear, and I love you back. The problem, my sweet friend, Carlo, is it's not in the same way." She stood on her toes and kissed his cheek. "Be happy, be well." She turned her back on him and walked away, head held high.

He stared after her. Laurel approached a minute later, her heels clicking unhappily on the tile floor. "What happened? Why is she leaving like that?"

"We're through," he said.

"What?" she gasped. "Why?"

"Because of you. She found out about the partnership."

"Go after her," Laurel directed.

"No. She doesn't love me."

Laurel huffed an exasperated breath. "She doesn't know what she wants, she never has. Go after her and talk her back into this."

He turned to face her. His expression revealed all he usually kept hidden from her, and she froze, shocked. "No. You don't know Bronwyn at all if you think she doesn't have a will or a head or a heart. I loathe you, and I always have. Stay away from me, I want nothing to do with you." He, too, turned and walked away, storming out of the banquet hall.

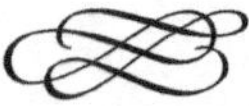

# CHAPTER 29

Bronwyn made her way across the ballroom to Julian who still sat alone at a table. His expression at her approach was a mix of amusement and concern.

"Is there a reason you're committing career suicide right now?" he asked.

"Yes."

"Are you going to tell me what it is?"

"Maybe. But first I have to ask you a question."

"Shoot," he said, and then put his hands up in case she had an actual gun.

"Did your fancy prep school teach you to dance?"

"Absolutely. But do you understand the full ramifications of what will happen if you and I dance together at this event?" he asked.

"Absolutely," she said.

"Well, then." He stood and extended his hand to her.

"Hold on a second, I'm about to heighten the drama." She reached up, unfastened her hair, and shook it out.

He whistled softly. "That was all kinds of sexy. Did I teach you that?"

"No, I think maybe it was innate." She put her hand in his and allowed him to lead her to the dance floor. Cameras clicked and reporters gathered in a huddle, falling all over themselves to get a shot of the two rival camps dancing together.

"All right, Bronwyn, you got me on the dance floor. Explain why you're committing political hari-kari."

"I was thinking about the animal kingdom."

"I'm in no way following your logic, but I trust this is leading somewhere good."

"Sometimes when an animal has a large litter, the mother pushes the runt aside, kicks it away repeatedly until the runt gets the idea and stops trying to feed. Usually when that happens, the runt dies. Sometimes it gets lucky and a bighearted someone comes along, scoops it up, gives it a home, and bottle feeds it back to health."

"I'm going to guess you fancy yourself the runt in this scenario," Julian said.

"Yes, and you're my someone. You found me at my lowest, picked me up, and brought me back to health. I can never thank you enough for that."

"Why does this feel like a benediction?" he asked.

"Maybe it is because the thing is, I'm in love with you. I know you don't see me that way, to you I'm just a friend, but grownup Bronwyn is in charge of her emotions, and she realizes it's healthy to tell the people you love that you love them, even when it's not reciprocated."

"Is that all?" he asked.

She nodded, her cheeks warm and flushed.

He took a shaky breath. "What have I ever done to make you believe I'm not in love with you?"

"You..." she started but stopped short. As she reviewed their time together, everything he had done had been an act of selfless love. "What?"

"Bronwyn, do you think it was an accident I appeared in that hedge when you were sixteen years old? Do you think I happened to be hanging around at the back of my property while my neighbors were having a party?"

"You went there to smoke, I thought."

"I could blow smoke in my mother's face and she wouldn't have cared less. I went there to watch you. I always, *always* watched you. Do you think my curse started when I became an adult? No. I could always read people, always see their hearts. And you had the biggest, softest, sweetest, and purest heart of anyone I'd ever encountered. It broke me to see you so sad, so alone, so unaware of how beautiful you are. And that day I couldn't take it anymore. Something compelled me over the hedge. You cried, and I kissed you. And it was as good as I'd always imagined. Better, maybe."

"But we never spoke again," she said.

"Because shortly thereafter I fell in love with drugs and alcohol, and addiction is a cruel and jealous mistress," he said.

She remembered something Carlo said then. "Did you and Carlo used to talk about me?"

"Endlessly. In fact I think our mutual adoration of you was the foundation of our friendship."

"Why didn't you tell me as soon as I came back?" she asked.

"You weren't in the right frame of mind for romance. All I wanted was to make you feel better."

She grasped his lapels, shaking him a little. "Why did you foist me on Carlo?"

He took her face in his hands. "Because, beloved, it was what you wanted."

"Of all the idiotic, self-sacrificing, rid…" She stopped talking. She had to because he was kissing her. She kissed him back, enthusiastically, and they became aware the group of reporters had turned into a horde, the dangerous kind that could soon get out of control.

Both their mothers' security teams stepped in and herded them out of the building, shepherding them around back to safety. Julian scanned the empty alley. "This is convenient." He settled his hands at her waist. "So your birthday is coming up."

"I'm not really into presents," Bronwyn said.

"Shocking. But I'd like to buy you something anyway."

"What did you have in mind?"

"A minivan. I was thinking I could get you good and pregnant, start filling it with that mini soccer team I plan to coach."

"You play soccer?"

"I'm rich, white, and went to prep school. You do the math. Of course I realize you have all those traditional family values, so I'd be willing to marry you and make an honest woman of you."

"It seems like I'm winning everything in that bargain," she said.

"Does it?" he asked. "Doesn't feel like it to me."

"I'd like to offer something in return," she said.

"I am all ears," he said.

"And hands and lips, apparently," she said as he bent to kiss her neck. "To expunge some of our white privilege and assuage your desire for social justice, I'd like to spend our lives giving back, really giving back, not just in name only."

"Do you want me to give away my trust fund? Because I'd have to get a job, and I don't actually have any skills," he said.

"Oh, you have skills," she said.

"Is that some kind of innuendo?" he asked.

"I fervently hope so," she said, drawing him to her for a kiss. A camera clicked beside them and they broke apart to see a reporter standing a foot away.

"Buddy, you mind? I'm trying to kiss my fiancée," Julian said. The guy's name actually was Buddy, and he often sold his work to Page Six of the *New York Post*.

"Fiancée? This is a goldmine," Buddy remarked. "Give me a statement. Come on, please, guys?"

Bronwyn sighed. "One statement, then leave us alone. On behalf of Congresswoman Baxter and Congresswoman Porter, we'd like to announce the engagement of our children, Julian Baxter to Bronwyn Porter. The small, private ceremony will take place at an unknown time and an unknown place. There will be no pictures for the public, and the press is not invited."

Buddy scribbled furiously as she talked, nodding. "Care to comment on the high likelihood this will end in divorce?"

Bronwyn opened her mouth, but Julian preempted her. "I'll take this one. Yes, we have a comment: your mom." He took Bronwyn's hand and, laughing, they made their way out of the alley and into the night.

# EPILOGUE

Julian finished his task and went to find his wife. She was on the floor, reading a picture book aloud to a group of rapt preschoolers. He stood at the back of the room, his heart awash in a fresh wave of adoration.

They had been married a year, and Bronwyn made good on her promise, volunteering them both to help at a local mission several days a week. She tended the preschoolers and, from the first moment, had found her niche in life. Bronwyn was made to love and be loved in return. Preschoolers sensed it the moment they met her, opening their hearts and arms to her at first sight. And she returned the favor, picking them up, cuddling, doting. The story ended, and Julian went forward to help her off the floor.

"Are you sure your back is up for this challenge?" she asked, peering up at him.

"You're weightless," he assured her, trying hard to hide his groan as he hauled her off the floor. She was hugely pregnant, her massively distended baby belly taking up all of her short waist and then some. "Would you like to visit the ducks before we leave?" The mission had a pond, and the pond had ducks.

"Do you even have to ask?" Bronwyn replied, wincing as she put a hand to her back.

"Okay?" Julian asked, trying to keep the anxiety out of his tone. It annoyed her when he hovered, but how could he not? She was ready to pop and still insisted on keeping her regular schedule.

"Fine. How was your class?"

"Horrible, ridiculously untalented and unmotivated. Their tiny little five-year-old fingers can barely hold the knitting needles. I expressed my displeasure and disappointment in them repeatedly because how else will they learn?" he said. Thanks to Bronwyn, he now spent his days teaching underprivileged children to do needlework, and he had never been happier or more fulfilled.

"Sounds like you need to bring my mom in for a guest lecture, see if she can use her select brand of criticism to get them on track."

"I'd love to because you know we're close, but she's so busy these days," Julian said. His mother had won the last election and then, after Bronwyn announced her pregnancy, declared it would be her last, due to her desire to spend time with her pending grandchild. Laurel, on the other hand, felt renewed determination to win her seat back, a task made harder by the leaked news of her affair exactly one week before the election.

"How's Louisa?" Julian asked. After initially blaming Julian for the leak, it came out Louisa was the one who'd sent the photos to the press. Angry at Laurel's interference in Bronwyn's relationship with Carlo, she had 'released the Kraken,' as Bronwyn liked to say, setting forth a treasure trove of Porter family secrets.

"She's good. She's decided not to look for a new place to work and to retire instead, as Carlo wanted."

"Ah," Julian replied. He took her hand and gave it a squeeze as they made the short walk to the pond. The baby ducks were out and swimming. They stood on the bank a while, watching in silence. Julian glanced down and did a double take. "Honey, did you step in a puddle? Your feet are soaked."

"Nah, my water broke," Bronwyn said.

"Let's go," he said, turning to head for the car. He took a few steps and realized Bronwyn wasn't beside him. "Can you not move?"

She shook her head.

"The pain's too bad?"

She shook her head.

He walked back to her and took both her hands. "Bronwyn, what's going on?"

"I don't think I can do this."

"Do what?"

"Have this baby," she said.

"I'll make sure you get the good drugs. If they refuse, I still have my old supplier's number. I'll get them off the street, I swear."

"It's not the pain, Julian. It's everything that comes after. What if I turn into her? What if I treat this baby like she treated me?"

"That's not going to happen."

"But what if it does? What if it creeps up on me, if the frustrations of motherhood mount until I snap?"

He rested his hands on her shoulders and looked in her eyes. "Honey, that's not you. You are not your mother. You are the polar opposite of your mother. You are kind and sweet and gentle and, most importantly, lacking ambition in every possible way, and I couldn't adore you more for it. There's another piece of the puzzle you're forgetting—me. I won't let it happen. If I feel things heading in that direction, I'll smuggle you to Canada and get you that therapy I've been threatening."

She frowned. "Why always Canada, Julian? The United States has one of the best…"

He pressed his palm to her mouth. "Save it for after the delivery, Abigail Adams."

She gripped his forearms, gasping as a contraction hit her. "Okay, now I'm afraid of the pain. Tell me more about drugs."

He put his arm around her and began herding her to the car. "Let me tell you about my good friend, opioids. You will be so blissfully strung out, you won't even remember my name."

"I will always remember your name, Evan," she said.

"Cute. Hey, at what point do you want me to call our families and tell them this is happening?"

"Sometime after the baby's fourth birthday," she said, gasping again as another contraction hit.

"Are you going to have this baby in our car? Because I just had it detailed."

"Depends on traffic," she said, bending over and moaning as she pressed her palms against the car. "They said it would take hours, but it feels like…" she broke off, groaning as a tidal wave of pain bent her in half again.

"Okay, new plan, back inside." There was a doctor and a nurse on duty at the mission. Julian took her to them while someone called an ambulance.

"I don't want our baby born at a mission," Bronwyn panted, sweat streaking her face.

"It's okay. Our baby will still be a privileged WASP, even if it's born here. I checked the constitution."

She laughed, but it ended on a sob as another contraction hit. "I don't think I can ever do this again," she said, clutching at him.

"Your mother did it six times. Are you going to let her beat you?"

She grabbed his shirt and yanked him closer. "Let's make it seven."

"There's my girl," Julian said, smoothing his hand over her sweaty forehead.

"And here comes your boy," the doctor said as Bronwyn started to push.

# ABOUT THE AUTHOR

Vanessa is a foodie who also loves to write. When she is not trying to find new ways to use sourdough, she likes to troll bakeries and taste test chocolate chip cookies. She lives in rural Ohio with her husband, children, and sheepadoodle. Her life's goal is to fill her books with enough coziness and sunshine to make someone smile. She would love to hear from you, drop her a line on email or facebook.

www.ingramcontent.com/pod-product-compliance
Lightning Source LLC
Chambersburg PA
CBHW031244210726

48287CB00003B/887